The Make-Believe Family

The Make-Believe Family

Darliss Batchelor

Word in Due Season Publishing, LLC

The Make-Believe Family

Darliss Batchelor

Copyright © 2018 by Darliss Batchelor
All rights reserved

Word in Due Season Publishing, LLC
P.O. Box 210541
Auburn Hills, Michigan 48321-0921

Cover Design by Cover Me Book Covers

ISBN 13: 978-0-9829686-5-9

Library of Congress Control Number: 2018908822

Printed in the United States of America

Acknowledgements

God is just awesome! I thank Him for gifting me to tell stories and aligning my life such that I can walk in it with ease. I love to tell the stories He gives me and am excited to continue on this journey with Him.

I must acknowledge my husband, Greg, for allowing me the grace to focus on my writing assignment. He has encouraged me when I didn't believe in myself and provided insight when I was unsure. I love and respect him for being who he is.

I must thank my pastors, John and Gale Stewart, and the Generation to Generation Ministries family for their love and support.

I want to thank the editor for this project, Kiera Northington. I look forward to working together again.

Renee Luke of Cover Me Book Covers, you are a lifesaver and a talented and gifted cover designer. Thank you for everything!

I thank LeTeisha Lucas for serving as a beta reader. I appreciate the time you took to read The Make-Believe Family and provide invaluable insight.

Last, but not least, I must acknowledge every literary supporter regardless of your contribution to my writing journey. Whether you read one of my books, offered a word of encouragement or recommended my books to others, I truly appreciate you.

The Make-Believe Family is dedicated to families everywhere.

Embrace, love and cherish each other.

Chapter 1

It was a beautiful summer day and the sunlight streamed through the window in the VIP room, turned bridal suite, at the Detroit church where Faith Richards would become Faith Lewis. The rays bounced off the crystal-encrusted lace overlay on her designer wedding dress, causing a display on the walls and ceiling of the space. Faith observed herself in the mirror. The sleeveless silk under-dress she wore sported a sweetheart neckline, a low-back, and a ball-gown-style skirt. Faith's toned arms and shoulders along with her tiny waist were on display.

Macie, Faith's best friend and maid of honor, gently removed the delicate creation from the hanger. "Are you ready to get into this?" Macie asked, moving toward her friend with the overlay.

"Yes, I guess I am."

The two were silent as Macie fastened the three buttons on the back of the overlay, leaving two peek-a-boo openings. Faith viewed herself in the mirror. A huge smile broke out across her face.

"I can't believe this day is finally here. I'm actually going to become Mrs. Jamison Lewis after all this time." Faith struggled with an errant piece of hair as Macie lifted her veil from the box.

"I can't believe it either after you almost messed up."

"Jamison and I are getting married, so that's all that matters. I think we can put the veil on now." The crystals glistened in the light as the two friends worked together to get the headpiece placed in just the right spot. Then, Macie helped her secure it in place.

Faith's mother, Vonda Richards, breezed into the room wearing a navy blue chiffon dress accented with rhinestones and set in silver at the neckline, wrists, and waist. Her salt and pepper hair was styled in her signature pixie cut.

"Are we ready in here, ladies? We're about five minutes out from the start of the wedding."

"We're ready, Mother. Just let me slip my shoes on and we can start. Are Jamison's parents here?"

"Yes, those snooty folks are here." Vonda glanced at her daughter. "Listen, we're not doing that today. This is your day. Don't pay them any mind."

As quickly as she entered, Faith's mother exited and her father, Bill Richards, entered.

"I'll wait outside." Macie followed Faith's mother out of the room.

Faith's father took a few moments to view his daughter. "You look absolutely breathtaking. Jamison is going to pass out." Faith and her father shared a hearty laugh.

"Thanks, Daddy. I was just telling Macie, I can't believe this day is finally here."

"Are you happy?"

"I'm ecstatic." Faith studied her father. "Why do you keep asking me that?"

"Because, it wasn't that long ago you were involved with someone else. I don't doubt Jamison is the right man. I'm just wondering how you got over your feelings for the other man so quickly."

Faith dropped her head. "I thought I had genuine feelings for Evan at the time. But, once I had some time to think, I realized that relationship couldn't work."

"I just don't want you to move on too soon. That can cause a lot of problems."

"Don't worry. I'm ready to marry Jamison."

"All right. We'd better get out there before your mother comes back in here." Laughter filled the room once again.

Faith stepped in front of the full-length mirror in the room. Her father stepped next to her and offered her his arm.

"I love you, Daddy."

"I love you, too, baby."

***

Boom! Tick, tick. Boom! Tick, tick. The bass and drum lines played as the bridal party introductions took place.

Faith and Jamison leaned their foreheads together as they awaited the announcement of their entry into the ballroom for their reception.

"I'm so nervous. I can't wait to see what you did with the ballroom decorations." Faith giggled as she leaned into her husband.

"You'll love it, baby."

"I don't know how you got me to give you full control of the reception. Now, I'm second-guessing myself."

Boom! Tick, tick. Boom! Tick, tick.

"I took it off your plate because it was stressing you out, woman. Now, trust me. It's awesome."

"They wouldn't even let me in when I stopped by here earlier."

"That's because I gave them strict instructions not to."

"And now! Everyone stand to your feet and put those hands together for the man and woman of the hour. The bride and groom. Mr. and Mrs. Jamison Lewis!"

The room erupted with applause and cheers as the doors swung open. Faith's hand covered her mouth as tears flowed down her face. Jamison took Faith by her other hand and led her into the room.

What seemed like thousands of blue, purple and clear crystals floated from the ceiling. The lighting was strategically placed to bounce off the jewels' facets, causing maximum sparkle. The tables were covered with glittery silver lace overlays covering purple tablecloths, with matching napkins and chair covers. Tall, bright-red floral arrangements sat at the center of each table.

Once she took everything in, Faith locked eyes with Jamison. "It's the room from my dream wedding notebook. How did you pull this off?"

"I hired the decorator from the magazine to recreate that room for us. All he did was change the colors and a few other tweaks."

"If this is what life with you is going to be like, I'm even more excited than I was. Thank you, baby." She leaned in for a kiss before she heard a familiar voice begin singing. Her head swung toward the stage to see Brian McKnight. Her jaw dropped as he began singing, "Everything."

Jamison took her hand and pulled her into him as the two began swaying to the music. When the song ended, the two continued moving to the non-existent beat until the wedding planner nudged them.

"Focus. Focus. You two can't check out yet. We still have a ways to go."

She led them to the table set up just for two in the front of the ballroom. The two gigantic white chairs graced with bling would be their table for the night.

After the crowd finished their dinner, the wedding planner escorted the newlyweds to a chair placed in the center of the dance floor. "It's time for the garter toss," she announced. "We'd like all the single men to come to the floor if you want to participate."

Faith and Jamison found their way to the dance floor. Faith sat on the chair and Jamison knelt in front of her. The music requested for this portion of the reception began playing. Faith lifted her dress up slightly to allow Jamison to find the garter belt more easily. As he slid his hands up her leg, he felt something he wasn't expecting.

"What's this?" he asked, wondering what he was feeling.

"Something you weren't supposed to find out about until later." Faith gave Jamison a devious look. He grinned in response.

"Well, I'm just going to pretend to be surprised later. Where do I find what I'm looking for?"

"The other leg, baby."

After the garter belt and the bouquet were thrown and the other traditional activities were completed, Jamison pulled his wife away from the crowd.

"I think it's that time." His voice was two octaves lower than usual.

"What time is that?" She playfully touched her nose to his.

"Don't play with me. You know what time."

"I'm not ready yet. I just want to soak up more of this love."

"I got some love for you to soak up." He pulled her out of the room after speaking with the wedding planner. Family and friends interrupted their partying to follow the couple outside and send them off the way they received them, with cheering and applause.

Once in the limousine, Jamison poured them both glasses of champagne. The newlyweds touched their glasses, linked their arms and sipped, all while keeping their eyes locked on each other.

"It was a long time coming but we're finally married." Faith snuggled closer.

"Yes, we are. Now we get to do married folks' things."

"Is that all you're thinking about?"

"Right now, yes." Faith smacked Jamison's hand. "Well, you asked."

Faith peered into Jamison's eyes. "I love you, Jamison."

"I love you more, Faith."

The newlyweds shared a deep kiss as the limousine pulled up to the luxury Detroit Foundation Hotel.

The driver exited the vehicle and opened the door for Jamison, who walked around the vehicle and offered his hand to help Faith out. They entered the hotel and checked in at the desk. Anticipation of the next phase boiled over as the two began exploring each other's bodies on the elevator. When they arrived at their suite, Jamison opened the door, freeing his hands to lift his bride and carry her into the room.

"Oh, you're carrying me over the threshold. I didn't know people still did that."

"I don't know what other people do, but my father taught me well."

As he placed her on her feet, Faith took in their room. A wall of floor-to-ceiling windows displayed a view of the city. The spacious room held tan micro suede sofas and chairs, flanked by end tables with coordinating lamps. To the right of the room's foyer was a huge bathroom, complete with a jetted whirlpool tub and rainfall showerhead. The suite screamed opulence and luxury.

Jamison took Faith's hands in his. "Does the room meet with your approval, Mrs. Lewis?" Faith's tears began to flow. "What's wrong, honey? Are you okay?"

Faith gathered herself and spoke, "Thank you for loving me, even when I wasn't sure about us. Thank you for your patience when I was indecisive and unsure. Thank you for fighting for our relationship, even when it wasn't clear which side I was on. I know that couldn't have been easy for you, but you persevered because you believed in us."

Jamison enveloped Faith in his arms for several moments. He grinned as he released her. He got down on his knees in front of her.

"What are you doing?"

Jamison dove under her dress. "I'm trying to see what I felt earlier. You know, that thing you told me I wasn't supposed to see until tonight." The two laughed heartily as Faith shooed him away and attempted to push her dress down.

Faith picked up her overnight bag and headed toward the master bath. "Just give me a few minutes to freshen up and change. I promise I'll reveal it to you. Okay?"

"Alright, girl. You know I've been waiting a long time. Don't keep me waiting too long, now. As a matter of fact, we can skip the lingerie," Jamison said, getting up from the floor.

"You are so silly. I'll be right back."

Faith pulled the traditional white long gown with its matching robe from her overnight bag. She held it up in front of her. It was beautiful but didn't quite match the mood she wanted to set for the night. She went back to the bag and pulled out the alternative ensemble. She was glad she'd decided to purchase something else, just in case. Her choice was clear.

She smiled as she thought about what transpired so far and what would happen before the sun rose in the morning. She freshened herself prior to pulling on her chosen lingerie for the night. She touched up her hair and makeup and exited the bathroom.

The suite was bathed in candlelight and the scent wafting from them added to the ambiance. Soft music played in the room.

"Hi, handsome," Faith said as Jamison dropped rose petals around the room.

He turned to view his wife. His mouth dropped open as his eyes ran up and down her body. The rest of the rose petals fell in a mound on the floor. Faith stood with her hand on one hip, wearing a lavender lace teddy with a plunging neckline, a matching sheer jacket, white patent leather thigh-high stiletto boots and rhinestone jewelry from the wedding.

"Well, all right," he said reaching out to her. She gripped his hand as he turned her around to get a full view. "I had no idea you had all this in you. I love it."

17

"There's a lot you don't know about me."

"I bet I'll start getting to know you tonight."

"I sure hope so."

Jamison backed up to the bed until he was sitting on the side of it, pulling Faith along with him. Faith pushed away from him with both hands. She turned her back to him and began to move to the music. Her hips dipped and swayed as the music flowed through her. She dropped to the floor until her bottom almost touched. She looked over her shoulder and seductively licked her tongue out as she unfolded herself and stood.

"Girl, did you just stick your tongue out at me?"

"Umm-hmm."

"I bet you won't come closer and do that."

Without a word, she stalked toward him. When she got close enough, she planted her hands on either side of him and stuck her tongue out again, almost touching his nose with it. He grabbed her and pulled her down on the bed.

The newlyweds laughed as their private wedding night festivities began.

Chapter 2

Faith and Jamison arrived at the hotel's Apparatus Room for breakfast, prior to heading to the airport for their honeymoon. The two were escorted to their table, handed menus and drink orders were taken. After ordering, Jamison motioned for Faith to place her hands in his. They smiled as they gazed into each other's eyes.

"Mrs. Lewis, are you ready for part two of our marriage celebration?"

"I am. But, I'm also curious about what you have planned for our honeymoon. Are you sure you won't let me in on where we're going?"

Jamison threw his head back and laughed. "Are you nervous?"

"A little. I guess."

"Didn't I do okay with the reception?"

"Yes, you did."

"Well don't worry about the honeymoon. Trust me. I got this. It's going to be great. Did you pack those swimsuits?"

"Yes, I did. Please tell me where we're going. I can't stand not knowing."

"You'll be alright," Jamison said as their waiter sat their meals before them.

After eating, they took a limousine from the hotel to the airport. Faith's mouth dropped as they arrived at a hangar holding a private jet. Jamison exited the car and took Faith's hand to help her out of the car.

"You have got to be kidding me," Faith said as Jamison led her toward the plane.

The pilot welcomed them aboard as the newlyweds' bags were loaded.

While Jamison spoke with the pilot, Faith whispered to the steward, "Where are we going?"

The man responded, "I'm sorry, Mrs. Lewis, but I'm not allowed to tell you. But, you're going to love it."

"I told you it was a surprise. Just relax. It's going to be okay," Jamison said, suddenly appearing after his conversation with the pilot.

Finally, the plane took off and five hours later, the pilot announced they were preparing to land. Faith looked out the window to see a large turquoise body of water. Obviously, this was the reason Jamison told her to bring plenty of swimwear.

"Baby, I'm going to ask you to trust me again," Jamison said as he waved a blindfold in the air.

She shook her head and said, "I don't think so."

"Why not?"

"I want to see what's going on."

The plane landed and the newlyweds stood to exit. Jamison held the blindfold up again. "I promise you won't miss anything important. I just want this to be a surprise."

Faith paused a few moments. "This better be good," Faith said as she allowed Jamison to place the cloth over her eyes. "I don't like all this secrecy." Jamison chuckled as he led Faith from the plane into the waiting Chevrolet Suburban that would take them to their destination.

Eventually, the vehicle came to a stop. "We're here," Jamison sang.

Faith reached for her face. "Good, I can take off this blindfold."

"Not yet, baby."

Faith and Jamison exited the vehicle and walked a short distance. When Jamison came to a stop, he removed the blindfold. Faith's eyes took in the sight before her.

"Whoa, this thing is huge!"

"It's a hundred-forty-foot yacht, to be exact."

"Where are we anyway?"

"We're in Providenciales, Turks and Caicos. This is our hotel while we're on our private Caribbean cruise. What do you think? Do you like it?"

Faith stood silently for a few moments before a smile spread across her face. "This is awesome, baby." Faith kissed her husband deeply before running into the vessel. As she surveyed the yacht, she noticed the custom-built Jacuzzi with the three-tiered waterfall, surrounded by a bar area which could seat twenty people at the various tables and couches. She went down a floor and into the massive master bedroom, which held a gray platform bed with dark wood trim, a matching writing desk, dressers and nightstands. Four large windows, a huge off-white couch and large mirror over the bed completed the room. As Faith continued her tour, she saw four additional bedrooms, a formal dining room, a movie room, various lounges and living areas, a waterslide and various water toys such as jet skis, kayaks, and underwater propulsion vehicles all onboard.

"This is so much to take in. Whose yacht is this?"

"It belongs to my friend, Jim. He loaned it and the crew to us for our honeymoon as a wedding gift. He even created the itinerary. Just so you know, he didn't even tell me where we're going, so we'll both be surprised."

"What are we going to do with all of this space?"

"We're going to relax and enjoy each other. That's what we're going to do."

Faith fell into Jamison and began to weep. She looked up at her husband and said, "This is beyond my wildest imagination. I don't know what to say. It's fabulous. I will never question your judgment again."

Jamison closed his arms around her. "I'm going to spend the rest of my life lavishing you with experiences I believe will make you happy. You will always know that I love and cherish you. You'll never have to worry about a thing."

Chapter 3

Faith ran to the kitchen to place the meal she'd picked up from her and Jamison's favorite restaurant on the counter, then rushed into the master bedroom to shower. Her daycare closed early, allowing Faith the preparation time she needed. She utilized the special shower gel and perfume Jamison bought her to wear for their wedding. She retrieved the bag she'd hidden under the bed a couple of weeks prior, put on the sexy lounge set and headed back down the stairs.

Tonight was a special occasion. It was their six-month anniversary. Faith took their formal china, silverware, and wine glasses from the cabinet and set the table in their dining room. She went about putting everything in place, including their tall crystal candelabras. Everything was set except the most important thing—her husband. She went to the family room to wait for him to arrive.

The marriage had been more than she could imagine. Jamison was more attentive than Faith thought possible after they almost lost each other in the "Evan" era. Romantically, he had been over the top. She was ecstatic she had officially become Mrs. Jamison Lewis.

"Hey, beautiful." Faith turned to see Jamison, arms full of flowers and gift bags.

"Hey, baby. I didn't hear you come in." Faith approached him and pecked him on the lips. Looking at the items in his hands, she asked, "Is all of this for me?"

"You know it's all for you." Faith helped relieve him of the items and placed them on the table.

"You're going to spoil me."

"That's my goal."

"Why don't you go upstairs and freshen up, while I put these flowers in a vase and get the food on the table."

"All right. It'll just take a moment." Jamison went to the master bedroom to freshen up and change into something more comfortable for the evening. As he entered the room, he heard Faith's cell phone vibrating on the dresser. He walked over to get a closer look. Seeing the name displayed, his investigative skills kicked in. He browsed the call log and noted a few conversations in the last week alone. "I don't like this," he said aloud. "But, I'm not going to let this mess up tonight."

"Are you talking to me?" Faith inquired from the dining room.

"I was just saying I'm going to take a quick shower and I'll be right down."

When Jamison returned to the dining room, Faith had set out platters full of seafood, various side dishes and a bottle of champagne was chilling.

"Come. Sit. Let's eat." Faith motioned toward the table. They both sat. Jamison blessed the food. Faith then prepared to serve Jamison first.

Jamison took Faith's hands in his. "I want you to know something. You are my queen and I honor you. You're worth more to me than anything or anyone else in my life. If you are ever unhappy, I will do whatever is necessary to fix it. You just say the word. Now, with that said, are you happy, my queen?"

Faith leaned toward him. "If I was any happier, I don't know if I could handle it." She brushed her lips across his and sat back. "Let me fix your plate before the food gets cold."

Jamison observed his wife as she went about dishing various items onto their plates. There was no indication she wasn't being true to him. But, he wondered why she was in contact with the person she was speaking to on a regular basis. Whatever was going on, he would find out. He was sure of it.

Chapter 4

Faith's phone rang, as she was folding laundry. For some reason, her body seemed extremely fatigued these days, but she didn't have time for it. Things still needed to get done and some of those things she had to make happen.

She picked up the phone and noticed it was Macie calling. "Hey, girl."

"Hey," Macie responded. "What are you up to?"

"I'm finishing up the laundry."

"Meet me at the sandwich shop. I haven't seen you since Christmas."

Faith thought for a minute and realized she hadn't eaten breakfast or lunch. She would probably feel more energetic if she got some food in her system. Since Jamison went to the office for a few hours, she decided she would get herself together to have a bite to eat with her friend. After all, she didn't get to hang out with her often since she and Jamison got married.

"Give me an hour and I'll meet you there."

Faith and Macie arrived at the restaurant at the same time, meeting in the parking lot. They greeted each other with a hug and walked in. The two settled into a booth as the hostess placed menus on the table in front of them. After a few moments, their server came to bring water and take their orders.

"So, how's Jamison?" Macie wondered, squeezing lemon into her water.

"He's wonderful. He's working for a little while today."

"So, looking at you, I don't have to ask how married life is treating you. You're glowing, girl."

"It's beyond amazing. I can't even tell you how wonderful it is."

"That's awesome. I'm glad to know there are some happily married folks. Are you sure Jamison doesn't have a brother or something? I want to glow, too." Faith yawned. "Not getting enough sleep?" Macie asked as a sly grin spread across her face.

"I think I might need some vitamins or something. That's all."

After a few moments, their waitress placed their orders in front of them. Faith blessed their meals and the two prepared to eat.

Faith scowled as she looked over at Macie's fish sandwich. "That fish smells awfully strong. Are you sure it's not spoiled?"

"It smells okay to me."

"Hmm."

"So, I didn't ask you to lunch just to eat. I have some news. I don't know how you'll feel about it. I don't even know how I feel about it yet."

"Girl, will you just tell me please?"

"Okay, you know I've been looking for new opportunities to advance my career." Macie took a napkin from the holder on the table and wiped her mouth and hands.

"Yes, did you find something?"

Macie nodded. "Yes, I did."

"That's a good thing. Why wouldn't I be happy about that?"

"It's in Atlanta."

Faith and Macie were silent for a few moments as Faith digested what Macie shared.

"You can't move to Georgia." Faith returned her sub to her plate and focused on Macie. "If you're in Atlanta, we won't be able to meet for lunch or go shopping or anything like that."

"I know, right? But, it's the perfect job. It provides a great salary and the perks are unheard of."

"But, what about us?" Faith motioned between the two.

"You have Jamison now. Besides, we'll only be a short plane ride away if I get the job."

Faith busied herself by picking up her sandwich and taking another bite. *Why did this job have to be four states away?*

"You're going to have to finish that fish sandwich because I can't hardly stand the smell of it." Faith got their waitress' attention and ordered a Coke.

"Since when do you drink pop?"

"It's just to help settle my stomach."

Macie's eyes narrowed. "Are you late?"

"Late for what?"

"You know...late."

"Oh, *that* kind of late. I don't think so. Why?"

"Because every time we come here, I always have a fish sandwich and you have never complained about the smell before. You're sitting here tired and needing vitamins and drinking Coke and stuff."

"What are you trying to say?" Faith shook her head and gestured with her hand for Macie to continue.

"Could you be pregnant, girlfriend?"

"No. I don't think so. We are very careful." A huge smile broke out on Faith's face. "Usually."

"That smile tells me all I need to know. I think you need to take a pregnancy test."

Faith leaned in and whispered, "You think so?"

Macie nodded. "Yeah, I do."

Chapter 5

Jamison arrived at his office suite hoping to have some quiet, uninterrupted time to focus on work. When he entered, he realized several of his employees had the same idea. His firm had grown exponentially after working on the high-profile case involving Janay Ingram. That was a difficult time for him, both professionally and personally. He was on the cusp of his one-man business exploding, which meant he had to do a lot of the work on his own at the time. The time required to maintain and grow his business took him away from Faith. Their relationship almost didn't survive and that gave Evan Ingram, Faith's former employer, room to move in on Faith. Yet, here he was, living his dream on both fronts. He was married to Faith and his business was on the verge of another surge in growth. He stopped, prepared a cup of coffee, then headed to his office.

He set his coffee down and shrugged off his bag. He sat in the large black leather chair behind the huge glass and metal desk. He booted up his laptop and opened the file for one of the cases he wanted to work on. As he looked over the information, his partner and close friend, Kardel Isaac, entered his office.

"Hey, boss. What are you doing here today? I thought you would be home enjoying your new wife."

"I thought I was going to have the office to myself this morning, but obviously that's not going to happen."

"Yeah, about that. Do you have a moment? I want to talk to you."

"Sure, have a seat." Jamison offered him a seat in front of his desk. "What's going on?" he said as he came around and sat next to Kardel.

Kardel rested one leg onto his knee. "Boss, people are feeling a little overwhelmed."

Jamison's eyebrows kissed. "Overwhelmed?"

"Yes. We're pedaling as fast as we can, but still unable to manage our workload. That's why all of these people are in here today. We're trying to get caught up."

"Are they working late during the week, too?"

"Those that can are."

"That can't happen." Jamison rested his chin on his folded hands for a few minutes, then rose from his seat. He headed toward the area where his employees were. He viewed the intake specialists that worked the phones, the researchers, and the rest of the team. How had he missed the fatigue and stress that was so palpable at the moment? He had to fix this.

"Can everybody just take a moment and gather around?" Jamison said as the team turned their attention to him. After everyone was within hearing range, he began to speak. "Good morning, everyone. I just had a conversation with Kardel, who shared some information with me. He tells me you all are overworked. I don't want you working like this to become the norm. Your relationships will suffer and that's not a good thing. So, I want each of you to stop whatever you're doing, pack up your things and go home. You'll all be paid for this morning. I'll see you Monday."

The number of employees present diminished quickly as they left to return to their homes and families.

Kardel approached him and said, "Aren't you heading out? I would think you'd want to get home to Faith."

"I'll leave in a few minutes. But, you and I need to sit down next week and look at what we can do to alleviate the necessity for so much overtime. Maybe some temporary contract workers would help get us over the hump. We can get some in here fairly quickly."

"Should I set up a meeting?"

"Yes, set aside a couple of hours and include the HR person."

"Okay, boss. I'll see you Monday."

Jamison thought about how he hadn't wanted to leave Faith this morning, but his business required additional time from him. He'd fallen back into his previous pattern of working too much. Though Faith still ran her day care, he carried the bulk of the financial responsibility. If he was going to continue doing that and perhaps add children to their family, it was necessary for the firm to continue expanding. He wasn't willing to change the standard of living for his household, unless it was to elevate it. Hopefully, the meeting next week would offer some answers for this good problem they had.

Chapter 6

Once all the children went home for the day, Faith went to the drugstore near their home to get the answer to a question that was running through her mind. She faced the wall of pregnancy tests. There had to be at least fifty different options available. *Which would be the most accurate? Should I use a dipstick or a test strip? Is it too soon to tell? Should I just go to the doctor?* She attempted to calm herself as all of these questions danced in her head.

Faith wondered if she was ready to be a mother. She was enjoying the one-on-one time with Jamison. They could just pick up and go on a weekend getaway whenever they desired. They didn't have to work around naptimes or feedings. Going to the movies would become streaming movies at home when they couldn't find a babysitter. However, seeing a tiny visible representation of her and Jamison's love would be amazing.

After studying the different brands, Faith picked up a variety of tests and placed them in her basket. If all the tests gave her the same result, she would be able to trust it. Her next stop was the vitamin aisle. She looked up and her eyes landed on those of Janay Ingram. This woman was somewhat of a friend to her at one time, because Faith was her children's babysitter. However, an unexpected relationship between Faith and Janay's husband, Evan, put a chill on the friendship. Faith could still see the effects of it in the woman's eyes. Faith noticed Janay had a pregnancy test in her hand as well.

Janay nodded her head. "Faith."

"Hello, Janay," Faith said. "How are you?"

"I'm well."

An uncomfortable and tense silence existed between the two women for a few moments.

"Janay, I never had a chance to apologize for what happened. I never meant to get involved with Evan like that. I hope you can forgive me."

Faith noticed Janay's face soften momentarily. "I see you and your husband are starting your family, huh. Congratulations."

"Thank you, but I don't know if I'm pregnant or not. That's kinda why I'm taking a home pregnancy test," Faith stated, waving the box.

Janay's scowl returned.

"You don't have to get smart with me. I know what a home pregnancy test is for."

"Then why did you ask me a question you already knew the answer to? I think you know the purpose for being in this aisle." Faith nodded toward the pregnancy test in Janay's hand.

Janay sauntered a little closer to Faith, who squared her shoulders and locked eyes with the woman.

"Knowing the kind of woman you are, you should probably pick up a home DNA test, too." Faith gasped. "You have a nice day."

Janay walked away and tossed the pregnancy test back on the shelf, leaving a shocked Faith with tears streaming down her cheeks. Why did that woman have to be so mean? Faith was no longer a threat to Janay and Evan, since she was married to Jamison. Faith assumed Evan and Janay were together as well. She decided the issue was not hers, but Janay's. She pulled herself together and headed for the vitamin aisle.

Chapter 7

Evan stood inside the front door looking for Janay, to arrive. It was her night with the girls and apparently, she was running a little late. The family had been through a lot over the past year and they were still working through some things. After everything that occurred with Janay's kidnapping and his emotional affair with Faith, Janay decided to leave the family home and move in with her mother, Big Momma and her sister, Cherlynn.

"When is Mommy going to get here?" Nahla, the oldest of their daughters asked. "Can I unzip my coat while we're waiting? It's hot."

"You can unzip it a little. I'm sure she'll be here shortly."

"Where did she go?"

"She had to go the doctor."

"Is her PPFC giving her problems again?" she asked.

Evan cocked his head to the side. "Her PPFC? What are you talking about?"

"You know. What Mommy got after that bad man took her and kept her away from us for a long time and Miss Faith was our mommy."

"Oh, you mean PTSD." Nahla nodded. "I don't know, Honey Bear."

Janay's car pulled up and she got out. She strolled to the door. Evan saw the sneer and the frown on her face. He'd seen this look before and knew she was locked and loaded to unleash her venom on someone. Since he was in her sights, he would probably be the recipient.

"Girls, I want you to go upstairs and play for a few minutes. I'll let you know when it's time for you to leave."

"But, Mommy just got here and we're all ready to go," Nia said.

"Mommy and Daddy just need to talk. It'll only be a minute. Now, do what I said, okay?" The three girls followed their father's instruction and went upstairs.

Janay entered the home without greeting her husband.

"Hi, Janay."

"Hi." Her one-word answer spoke volumes.

"What's going on? You seem upset."

Janay folded her arms across her chest. "I saw your little girlfriend, Faith, at the drugstore."

"You know she's not my girlfriend."

"She was buying a pregnancy test. Do you know anything about that?"

"No, I don't. Why?"

"I was wondering if you might be her baby's father."

Evan rolled his eyes and said, "There's no way I could be her child's father, Janay. So, you can relax."

"No. No," she said, wagging her finger as she moved toward him. "See, if you hadn't hooked up with her in the first place, we wouldn't be dealing with all of this mess."

"I shouldn't have allowed myself to get involved with her. But, I wasn't responsible for everything that happened."

Janay looked away. "Just when I make progress with therapy, something always happens to set me back." She returned her gaze to Evan. "Sometimes, I think I hate you for what you did to me. For what you did to us. I don't know if we can ever recover."

"I'm sorry, babe." He took Janay's hands in his. "I hope we'll be together on the other side of this. But, if we don't, I want you to know I love you more than I did the day we got married."

"I remember our wedding like it was yesterday." She looked into his face.

"I remember your father looking like he wanted to fight me."

The couple laughed.

"Yeah, he felt like you were taking his little girl from him and he wasn't ready for that." The duo laughed once again.

"We barely had a dime, but we had so much love for each other."

"Money didn't matter then. We were just happy to be together in that rickety little apartment." Janay smiled at the fond memories. Then, the frown returned as she pushed Evan away. "Don't think just because we're going down memory lane that everything is okay. It's not."

Evan backed away. "Girls, come on down. It's time for you to go." The Ns , as they were affectionately referred to at times, came down the stairs and ran into their mother's arms.

Nahla held her mother's hand but looked into her father's eyes. "Are you happy, Daddy? You look sad."

"Don't worry about me, Honey Bear. I'm okay. You girls have a good time with Mommy. I'll see you tomorrow."

Janay directed the girls to the door. She glanced over her shoulder at Evan as she left the house.

Evan watched as the car holding his family disappeared from his view. The months since Janay decided she needed space were unsettling for him. There was once a lot of love in this place. When the Ns were with their mother, the house felt empty. Lonely. He didn't want to live the rest of his life this way, but he had no idea how long it would take Janay to decide what she wanted to do.

Janay begged him to choose her and the Ns when he was forced to choose between them and Faith. He'd chosen his family, then Janay decided she wasn't sure if she wanted to be with him anymore. He'd tried to return to Faith, but she rejected him, and

Janay still didn't want him. Janay moved out and that's where they still stood.

He thought about what Janay said about Faith being pregnant. He hadn't thought about Faith in months. But, now that Janay had mentioned her, thoughts about her flooded his mind. Their relationship had been key for him while Janay was missing. She was a wonderful support and friend, who he thought could have become something more. He shook his head. He couldn't get too caught up in reminiscing about Faith. It was unproductive. He decided to focus his complete attention on his relationship with Janay.

He looked at his watch and decided he would go see a movie and get some dinner. He pulled up the movie schedule on his phone and decided to see the new action film that had just come out. That would fill some of his time and keep his loneliness at bay, at least for a few hours. He took his jacket from the coat closet and left the house.

Chapter 8

Jamison answered the personal phone line established solely for Faith and his family. He was in the middle of an important meeting but since it was Faith, he decided to step away from the conference room briefly to take the call.

"Hey, sweetness," he said.

"Hey, honey," Faith purred. "Do you have a few minutes?"

"I have all the time in the world for you."

"What time do you think you'll be coming home today?"

"We're busy, baby. It's going to be a while before I get out of here."

"Look. I know there's a lot going on with the firm and that's important. But, tonight, I need you to come home a little earlier."

"Is something wrong? Are you sick?"

"No, it's nothing like that. I just really need you here. I have a Valentine's Day gift for you."

"You need me?" Seduction dripped from his voice.

"I do."

"Give me an hour."

"I'll be waiting for you."

Jamison and Faith disconnected their call. Jamison re-entered the conference room.

"My lady just called and asked me to come home, so you know that's what I'm going to do. Can you finish up here?"

"Sure." Kardel stood and approached the front of the room. "I can do that, boss."

"Try to be done within the hour and then everybody go home."

"Oh, we can definitely do that," Kardel said. "Don't worry about this. I can handle it."

***

Thirty minutes later, Jamison walked into their house. He entered through the mudroom and placed his work bag and coat in the closet. He pushed the door open and saw Faith sitting on the couch asleep. She looked ethereal with her hair styled in a curly halo on top of her head. Her skin seemed to shimmer from the light emitting from the television. The fact she was sleeping caused him to exhale. Though she told him everything was okay, he wondered if that was true since the moment she called him. She stirred when he planted a soft kiss on her forehead. Her eyes were slits as she began to wake up.

"Faith," he said, sitting on the couch next to her and taking her in his arms. "I'm home."

"I must've fallen asleep."

"You did."

Faith cuddled closer to Jamison and appeared to be going back to sleep.

"Hey, you asked me to come home and now you're going to sleep on me?"

"I'm sorry. It's almost like I can't keep my eyes open."

"Are you going to tell me what's going on?"

"Yes."

"Okay. I'm listening."

She looked up at him with somewhat hooded eyes and smiled.

"You're going to be a father. I'm pregnant."

Jamison's mouth dropped open and his head fell back. Tears began to flow and a smile appeared. He lowered his head, then took her face in his hands and allowed his lips to linger on hers. He sat staring at her for several moments, then pulled her close.

"Aren't you going to say something?"

"I don't know what to say. I'm feeling so many different emotions."

"Are you happy?"

"I'm ecstatic." Jamison placed his hand on her belly. "I can't believe you're carrying our child."

"I still have to go to the doctor for confirmation." Faith jumped up and like a flash, she moved toward the bathroom.

"What's wrong?" Soon after, Jamison heard why Faith left so quickly. "Let me get you some saltine crackers. I hear that helps."

Chapter 9

Jamison and Faith moved between their kitchen and dining room, setting the table for dinner with family and friends. Once everything was on the table, Faith inspected to ensure everything was just right. The various salads, grilled chicken, salmon, rolls and fruit made for a colorful display. Everything had to be perfect for this occasion. Her in-laws were coming, along with close friends, Kardel and Macie. Her parents would be Skyped in from California at the appointed time.

"Is everything set?" Jamison asked as he placed his arm around her and rubbed her belly with the other.

"I think so. All we're waiting on now is for everyone to arrive." Faith wrung her hands, then went over to the table and adjusted a plate.

Jamison walked over to her and grabbed her by the shoulders. She turned toward him. "Hey. Everything is going to be fine."

"If you say so." Faith wrapped her arms around herself.

"I say so. Now, I want you to get off your feet." He led her to the adjoining great room and waited for her to sit on the couch. "Do you need to put your feet up?"

"No, I'm okay. Thank you, honey."

The doorbell rang, announcing the arrival of their first guest. Jamison answered the door to find Macie and Kardel. The two entered the home and greeted Jamison.

"Sooo, who is this fine man I found on your porch?" Macie smiled at Kardel and inspected him from top to bottom.

"This is Kardel Isaac, my business partner, and college buddy. Kardel, this is Faith's best friend, Macie King."

Kardel brought Macie's hand to his lips and kissed it. "Glad to meet you, Macie." Macie giggled.

"Wait. You two haven't met before?"

"No, I believe I would remember that," Kardel said, with his eyes locked on Macie's.

Faith appeared at the door. Hey, you two." Neither of them looked at her. She smiled as she observed the interaction between Macie and Kardel. "Let's have a seat while we wait for Jamison's parents."

About ten minutes later, the doorbell rang again, announcing the arrival of Hendrix and Davore Lewis. Jamison's mother wore a black tailored pantsuit with a print tank. Her red-bottomed pumps and designer handbag completed her look. Her dark hair flowed in soft curls and her makeup was flawless. Jamison's father's salt and pepper hair was lined perfectly as if he'd just left the barber.

He wore a cream linen sport coat, dark chocolate pants, and a tan shirt open at the neck.

Faith looked down at her dark denim jeans, white button-down shirt and slippers, and felt out of place in her own home. Jamison sensed her uneasiness and pulled her close.

"Hey, Mom. Dad. How are you?"

"We're well," Jamison's father said shaking his son's hand. Then, he tilted his head in his daughter-in-law's direction. "Faith."

"Hi, Hendrix and Davore." Faith shrunk further into Jamison.

"Mom and Dad, you remember Kardel, don't you?"

"Certainly. Hi, Kardel. It's good to see you again," Davore said.

"This is my friend, Macie. You saw her at the shower and the wedding."

"Hi, Mrs. Lewis." Macie slightly nodded.

Davore smiled, though it didn't quite register in her eyes. "Yes, I remember."

Macie rolled her eyes.

"Everyone, let's have a seat. Dinner is ready." Jamison directed everyone toward the dining room.

After Jamison blessed the meal, the group ate. Afterward, Macie and Faith put the leftover food in the refrigerator and cleared the table. As Macie rinsed each dish and Faith placed them in the dishwasher, Macie asked, "Kardel is fine. Girl, why have you been holding out on me?"

"He was at the wedding. You didn't scope him out then?"

"I was focused on getting you safely down the aisle."

Jamison entered the kitchen. "Baby, are you almost done in here? I'm going to get your parents on."

"Yes, go ahead and connect with them. We'll be there in a minute."

Once everyone was settled in the family room and Faith's parents were Skyped in, Jamison began to speak.

"Loved ones, as you probably guessed, we didn't just invite you here for dinner. We have something to tell you all."

Jamison motioned for Faith to stand next to him. She placed a tray holding a bottle of sparkling cider and chilled flutes on the coffee table. She then stood next to Jamison. He placed his arm around her. She looked up at him and smiled.

"This gorgeous woman standing next to me has made me happier than I ever thought possible. It was confirmed a few days ago that she is carrying our first child."

Macie and Kardel, along with Faith's parents clapped, cheered and hugged the couple, while Hendrix and Davore glanced at each other with blank faces.

Jamison's eyes landed on his parents and the smile he had on his face just seconds earlier disappeared. "Mom. Dad. Did you hear what I just said? You're going to be grandparents."

Davore and Hendrix glanced at each other. "We're happy. But, you two haven't even been married a year yet. A lot of things can happen in the first year, son." Hendrix's face showed concern.

"What?" Faith asked her father-in-law.

"You know what!" Davore pointed her finger at her daughter-in-law, who backed away in response.

Jamison positioned himself in front of his wife. "Baby, I got this. I don't want you to get your blood pressure up." Jamison's attention returned to his parents. "Go ahead and finish what you were saying."

Davore rushed toward Jamison and grabbed his hands. "We just feel like you should've waited a little longer, son, to make sure things are going to work out."

"So, where would you get the idea it wouldn't work out?" Again, Davore and Hendrix glanced at each other. "I'm insulted you would even imply we won't make it. This was supposed to be a happy occasion, but somehow it turned into something different. I think the two of you should leave. I don't want my wife to get more upset. Because if something happens to that baby, because of the two of you... we don't want to think about that." Jamison walked through the foyer to the front door, with his parents following.

Davore turned around and pleaded with Faith. "I'm just concerned about my baby. You'll understand when you have yours." She then turned and joined her husband as they exited.

After a few moments, Jamison returned to the family room, interrupting the conversation being held between Kardel, Macie, Faith and her parents. He knelt in front of Faith and said, "I don't know what that was all about, but my parents were way out of line. We'll deal with this later. But, make no mistake about it, I will not allow anyone to cause you or this baby any harm. I'm not going to have it."

"Well, all right then, Jamison," Macie said, snapping her fingers, causing the room to erupt in laughter. "I'll pour this sparkling cider so we can get this party started."

Jamison pulled Faith up from her seated position and enveloped her in his arms. Faith felt loved and protected in a whole new way. However, her mind wandered to her in-laws and what their issue was. What could they have against her?

Chapter 10

Macie and Faith parked their car and went into the mall. Today's visit was necessary, since Faith's clothes were fitting more snugly.

"Girl, I'm running out of bottoms with elastic in the waist. I'm so uncomfortable, I just can't take it anymore," Faith said, lifting her top just above her waistband. "Look at this."

"I noticed. Aren't you still a little early to be showing like that?" Macie pointed at Faith's middle.

"I don't know. All I know is it's time for some maternity clothes."

The friends walked in silence for a few moments.

"How is Jamison? I know he must be vibrating with excitement."

"He's so excited. He wants me to stop working. He thinks it might be too much for me."

"How do you feel about that?"

"I think it's too soon to stop working. He won't let me do my aqua aerobics. He's even watching everything I eat. I appreciate that he cares, but he needs to let up a little. I can't live in a bubble for the rest of this pregnancy. It's a bit much, you know."

"One thing I know for sure is that man loves you. He believes he's doing the right thing for you and this baby. I don't know a woman alive who wouldn't appreciate that."

The ladies walked into the specialty maternity store and began to look around. Faith found a few pairs of pants, a couple pairs of leggings and some dresses to try on. Macie sat outside by the three-way mirror, waiting for Faith to model each item. When Faith came out in one of the dresses, Macie asked, "Did Jamison ever speak to his parents about what happened at the pregnancy announcement dinner?"

Faith exhaled. "Strangely enough, they haven't called him at all since that happened. He told me he's going over there today. He thought it was best to take some time to cool off before he talked to them about it."

"I don't know how you deal with them. If it was me, I would've let them have it." Macie shoved her fist into the palm of her hand.

"I decided to let him handle it. That's the way he wanted to do it."

"Have they been like that with you all along?"

"They haven't been the friendliest, but I didn't know they had some trepidation about us getting married. Jamison said it took him by surprise, too." She viewed herself in the dress from all three angles. "What do you think about this dress?"

Macie stood and shifted the belt on the dress Faith was wearing. "That is so cute on you."

"I think I'll get this one for sure." Faith moved toward the dressing room.

"You should."

***

Jamison had so many thoughts swirling around in his head as he pulled into the gated community where his parents lived. The spacious estates were a testament to hard work and solid money management. The curved streets mirrored Jamison's emotions. On the one hand, he loved and respected his parents. He knew the depth of the sacrifice his parents made for each of their children when necessary. He was keenly aware of how much they loved their children. However, Faith was his priority now. As her husband, he was charged with not only loving and respecting her, but also protecting her. He cherished and took his role seriously. Balancing his relationship between his parents and his wife was new for him. He was sure he would master it. It would just take time, and overcoming this first challenge in the process was key.

His parent's lack of excitement about the new grandchild concerned him. More than that, their reaction disappointed him. Questioning the stability of his marriage angered him. It was necessary for him to know where they were coming from and he wouldn't leave until he did.

He parked his car in the circular driveway which held twenty cars when they hosted parties. He said a prayer prior to exiting, asking God to help him remain calm and respectful. The huge carved wooden door opened before he stepped onto the porch. He looked into the sad eyes of his mother.

"I knew you'd come. I just didn't think it would take this long. Come on in." Jamison frowned upon hearing her monotone voice. She lifted her arms to embrace him, then dropped them to her side. He reached for her, giving her a quick tentative hug. "Your father is in the library. Would you like something to drink? I was just on my way to the kitchen."

"No, but thank you for asking, Mom."

"You don't have to be so formal. We are still family," she said. "I'll be there shortly."

Jamison and his mother parted ways as he walked through the home headed toward the library where he found his father.

Jamison stood at the double doors of the library entrance observing the man he'd looked up to his entire life. He was focused on whatever he was looking at on his laptop. He hummed along to the traditional jazz music that flowed through the room. Jamison adored this man.

"Hey, Dad." Jamison announced his presence.

Hendrix spun around in his desk chair and removed his reading glasses from his face. "Hey, son." He stood and gestured for Jamison to take a seat. "How are you?" He offered his hand to his son for a handshake. Jamison obliged him.

Shortly afterward, Davore entered the room carrying her coffee cup and sat next to her son. The silence in the room was tangible. Davore sipped her tea. Hendrix fiddled around with stuff on his desk.

"Somebody want to tell me what's going on?" Jamison asked, breaking the silence.

Davore and Hendrix looked at each other. "I'll say it," Davore began.

Hendrix held up his hand and said, "No, I think this needs to be handled man-to-man."

"Okay, Dad. I'm listening."

"Let me just get right to it. Are you sure Faith really loves you?"

"What kind of question is that? Of course she loves me. She's my wife."

"It's awfully beneficial being your wife, too. Isn't it?" Davore pointed at her son.

"I thought I was going to do this."

Davore nodded. "You're right. I'm sorry. Carry on." She took a sip of her tea.

"We're just wondering if she would feel the same way if things were different."

"We think she's using you," Davore interjected, then set her cup down on a nearby table.

"In a nutshell, we think she loves all you do for her."

"Say what, now?"

"I think she's in love with that Evan. He couldn't give her the lifestyle she desired, though, Davore said.

"Look, you fell in love with Faith. You gave her way too much too soon. You let her live in that house rent-free, while she dated another man. You couldn't even trust her to stay faithful to you while you were engaged. You built that big, beautiful custom house over there you two just moved into. Now, she's conveniently pregnant. I'd call that an insurance policy." Hendrix used air quotes. "What if you couldn't do all of that? Would she still be with you?"

Jamison's eyes widened. He fell back in the chair and shook his head slowly. "That is the most ridiculous thing I've ever heard. First, how could you know what Faith does or doesn't do that shows her love for me? You have no idea. Second, you two don't get to judge our love. Third, how did you guys come up with all of this?"

"We've just been paying attention to what's been happening. You've been so busy being in love, you haven't been able to see it."

"I think you two are being nosey. You're just looking for a reason to dislike Faith."

"We don't like how she treated you. We're your parents. You can't blame us for being concerned."

"I'm going to say this to the both of you once. So, I want you to listen closely. You're going to have to accept the fact that Faith is my wife, whether you deem her worthy or not. I suggest you both figure out how to respect her too, because the last thing I'm going to do is allow anyone to disrespect my wife. So, I'm going to leave now. I love you both. But, I'm serious about what I said." Jamison stood, along with his parents. He hugged them and left their home.

***

Jamison rode around for an hour after leaving his parent's home. He couldn't believe the fairytale his normally logical parents made up to justify their dislike of Faith. But, what was the real problem? Did he miss something?

His parents had always made Faith uncomfortable, because of their often high-brow attitudes. Faith never mentioned it, but her body language indicated they made her uncomfortable. However, Jamison never doubted that the relationship would improve and become more relaxed over time. It appeared his expectations were unreasonable.

He knew Faith was going to ask him what his parents had to say. The truth was Jamison didn't believe they shared their true concerns with him. Sharing what they did say would probably cause Faith to react negatively. How was he going to handle it? He decided he would just be honest with the woman and hope she would be forgiving when his parents changed their attitudes.

Jamison pulled his vehicle into his driveway and engaged the garage door opener. Faith's vehicle was already parked there meaning she'd returned from her shopping spree with Macie. He smiled as he thought about her need for maternity clothing. He loved the way she looked normally, but pregnancy made her look heavenly. Her skin glowed, her hair was growing and her belly was expanding. All wonderful signs of the miracle happening inside her body.

He pulled out his cell phone to check Faith's phone records. He checked from time to time. After the conversation with his parents, he felt he needed to check her phone log once again. He dropped the phone back into his lap before logging into the app. He didn't feel right spying on her. Curiosity got the best of him and he picked it up and signed in. He waited a few seconds for the data to load. Once it did, he frowned. He turned his phone off and headed inside.

Faith met him as he entered the family room. "Hey, honey." She stood on her tiptoes and pecked him on the lips. She backed up from him for a moment, observing the expression on his face. "How did things go with your parents?"

"I'll tell you in a minute. First, I want to hear about shopping. Did you find some things that are as beautiful as you?" Jamison asked, leading Faith to the couch.

Faith hesitated before she responded to his inquiry. "I probably got more than I need, but I can't run around naked, you know." She shrugged.

"Why can't you? I wouldn't mind," he said, leaning in for a kiss. They both laughed.

"Sooo..."

"What?"

"Your parents."

"Okay. Here's the deal. They think you're taking advantage of me."

"What?" Faith looked at her husband with a single lifted eyebrow. "Were they drinking brandy or whatever rich people drink?"

"No, baby." He chuckled. "But, I told them I won't tolerate them disrespecting or mistreating you in any way."

"How am I supposed to feel, knowing they think I'm taking advantage of you? Now, I'm going to be even more uncomfortable around them, thinking they're watching my every move."

"You just be you. It's up to them to fix this. I'm telling you, it won't work any other way and they understand that."

Faith thought for a moment. Though she wondered what caused her in-laws to feel this way, she wasn't sure she wanted the details. It could only make things more difficult.

"I won't lie and say this news doesn't upset me. And things will be kinda awkward and tense until things shake out. But, if they're willing to make amends, I'll try to work with them."

"That's not all."

"There's more?"

"Yeah. I think you need to know everything. They mentioned the situation with Evan, too."

"Evan? I haven't spoken to Evan in forever. What's their concern with him?"

"Are you sure you haven't spoken to Evan recently?"

"No, I haven't." She looked at Jamison and did a double take. "Don't tell me you believe them."

"We promised we'd be completely honest with each other even if it hurt, right?"

"Right. I haven't spoken to Evan."

"I know you've been talking to him."

"How would you know if I've been talking to him?" Jamison looked at her, but didn't respond. "Oh, my goodness. You've been checking my phone calls?" She shook her head. "I can't believe you. You don't trust me."

"I do trust you. Your phone was laying on the dresser one day and I saw his name come up on your caller ID. I looked at your call log and noticed there were other phone calls from him. I became suspicious and I've checked a couple of times since then. So, you can't tell me you haven't had contact with him. The question I have is why."

"I know you're a private investigator and everything, so your instincts are to check everything out. But, did you ever think to just ask me?"

"No, I didn't." Jamison dropped his head. "That didn't occur to me at the time."

Faith reached over and lifted Jamison's face with her hand. "I am so mad with you right now."

Jamison lightly rubbed her belly. "Don't upset the baby."

"You'd better be glad I'm pregnant because otherwise I would really let you know how I feel. Now, I have not been talking to Evan. I've been talking to Nahla and sometimes Nia. They're too young for cell phones, so Evan allows them to use his. Okay?"

Jamison dropped his head once again. He gathered her hands in his. "I am so sorry I ever doubted you. Please forgive me for accusing you of talking to Evan. I should have known better."

"Yes, you should've known better. I forgive you, but next time just ask me."

Her cell phone rang and Evan's name appeared on the display. Faith answered, putting the call on speakerphone.

"Hi, Nahla."

"Hi, Miss Faith." It was Evan and Janay's oldest daughter. The girl was very attached to Faith since she'd been the family's childcare provider since Nahla was born. Faith didn't discourage Nahla's desire to stay in contact with her and she wasn't sure she should cut the young girl off.

"Hi, Nahla. How are you and your sisters?"

"We're fine. Nia and Naomi bug me all the time. Mommy and Daddy said they'll grow out of it." Faith chuckled, hearing the typically sensitive Nahla speak about her little sisters that way. "Me and the Ns really miss you. Can we come over? We'll be good."

"I don't know, honey. You remember I told you I got married, right?"

"Yes."

"Well, that means I have to spend time with my husband."

"But, that doesn't mean you can't see us sometime, too. Right?" Nahla was not letting Faith off the hook.

"You know what? You're right. We have to get permission from your parents, though. You understand?"

"Yay! I'm going to talk to Daddy right now. I'll call you back when he says yes."

"Okay, but not tonight."

"Bye, Miss Faith."

"Bye, Nahla."

"I don't think it's healthy for her to still be connected to you like that, especially with the baby coming," Jamison said.

"I've been in her life since she was born. How do I just tell her we can't talk to each other anymore?"

"What are her parents saying?"

Faith gave Jamison the side-eye. "You want me to call Evan and ask him?"

Jamison paused for a few seconds. "You've got a point."

"She'll probably lose interest in talking to me as she gets older anyway. Enough about that." Faith looked Jamison in the eye. "Are we okay?"

"Yes. We're good."

Chapter 11

Faith pulled on her thick socks, sweatshirt, and sweatpants and headed to the family room. She took the ponytail holder from her wrist and used it to hold her curls in a high bun. The Detroit Pistons were playing a big game tonight and snacks were a must. She stopped in the kitchen to plate the nachos, wing dings, French fries, and chocolate chip cookies they would snack on during the game. She poured a glass of Kool-Aid for Jamison and grabbed a bottle of water for herself.

"Jamison, can you come help me carry these snacks, please? I don't want to miss the tip-off."

"I'm on my way."

Jamison showed up next to his wife. He smiled as his fingers played in her hair.

"You are so sexy without even trying."

She ran her hand over his head. "You're pretty sexy yourself."

They got the snacks on the coffee table just before the game began.

During the first commercial break, Faith asked her husband, "Have you talked to your parents since you had the conversation?"

"I talked to my father for a few moments. They seemed to be more excited about the pregnancy."

"Hmm... Do you think they're really happy?"

"I don't know, but it's a start."

Faith's phone rang and she showed its screen to Jamison. The caller ID said it was Evan. Jamison nodded and she answered the phone in speaker mode.

"Hi, Nahla."

"Hi, Miss Faith. I can't talk long because I have to go to bed soon."

Faith chuckled. "Okay, baby. Is everything all right?"

"Yes, I was calling to ask you a question."

"What is it?"

"Well, me and Nia are going to be in a dance recital. Can you come?"

Faith looked over at her husband. "I don't know, honey. When is it?"

"Just a minute."

"Okay." A few moments passed.

"Hi, Faith." Hearing Evan's voice startled Faith.

"Hi, Evan."

"Look, uh, Nahla and Nia really want you to come to their recital. That's all they've been talking about. We wanted to give you plenty of notice. Do you think you can make it? They would love it if you could."

"I'll think about it. I have to talk to Jamison to see how he feels about it, too. Text me the details."

"Okay, I will." A moment of silence passed. "How are you?"

Jamison spoke up before Faith could respond. "All right, Evan. Faith said she'll think about the recital. We need to get back to the game. Good night." Jamison took the phone and ended the call, then turned his attention to Faith. "It's one thing for you to stay in touch with the Ns, though I'm not so sure that's wise. But, it's another thing for you to be talking to Evan. I'm not going to have that. So, if that means you have to disconnect from the Ns to keep that from happening, then that's what you're going to have to do."

Faith didn't respond for a few moments. Finally, she sat up and turned toward Jamison. "I'm a grown woman and I'll talk to who I please. You have to trust me not to do anything detrimental to us." She waved her hand between the two of them. "If I choose to stay in touch with the Ns, I'm not going to have you telling me I can't."

Faith left the room. She entered the bedroom and slammed the door. The Pistons game night celebration was over.

***

Nahla jumped around in front of her father. "What did she say? Is she coming?"

"She said she would think about it. We'll just have to wait and see what happens."

"I think she'll come. She still loves us. Right, Daddy?"

"Yes, Honey Bear. She still loves you." Evan fidgeted with the phone. "Go ahead and get ready for bed. I'll be there in a few minutes to tuck you in."

"Okay, Daddy." Nahla bounced out of the room with a huge smile on her face. It seemed Faith still had that effect on her. Evan was surprised at how hearing Faith's voice impacted him as well.

Chapter 12

Jamison lumbered into the office later than his normal time of arrival. Last night's celebration ended in Faith storming to their bedroom where he found her feigning sleep. When he arose, Faith was still asleep so he chose not to wake her. It was difficult for him to sleep when he couldn't spoon with her. Touch her. Smell her hair.

He entered his office after getting a cup of coffee and fell into his seat. Moments later, Kardel came in as well.

"Good morning." He scrunched his nose. "I think."

"It's a good morning. I'm just a little tired. That's all." He yawned, then took a sip from his cup.

"Everything all right?"

Jamison leaned back in his seat, crossed one leg over the knee of the other and positioned his hands under his chin. "Faith and I had a disagreement last night."

Kardel chuckled. "She didn't make you sleep on the couch, did she?"

Jamison laughed. "No, nothing like that." He leaned over his desk. "Close the door please." Kardel obliged and returned to his seat.

"I found out Faith has been talking to the girls she used to babysit."

"That's not a problem for you, is it?"

"It is when Evan gets on the phone and tries to start a conversation with my wife."

"Aww, man. I know you're not worried about him."

"No, I trust Faith."

"Well, what was the argument about?"

"I forbade her from talking to him."

"I've never been married, but I've been in enough relationships to know not to forbid a woman to do anything."

"It bothers me that he's still hanging around. I want him to go away."

"Have you said that to her?"

"No, I just basically told her it wasn't allowed."

"I agree with the sentiment. I wouldn't want my wife in regular contact with her ex. But, sometimes it's not what you say but how you say it. You need to go home and finesse this better. Stop by the jewelry store or something and communicate with the woman. I bet you'll get some sleep tonight."

"For someone who's never been married, you have a lot of wisdom in this area." Jamison thought a moment. "Can you handle things today?"

"Yeah, boss."

"I think I'm going to leave. I'm not going to be productive today anyway."

"Don't worry I got this. Go home and fix things with Faith."

"Thanks, bro. I'll see you tomorrow." Jamison retrieved his bag and coffee and left.

***

Faith curled her feet underneath her on the couch. She and Jamison had agreed she would schedule a break for her daycare this week, giving her some time off. She enjoyed watching TV shows she didn't normally get to see. She had a day of beauty planned for herself later in the week including hair, nails, pregnancy massage and facial. If Jamison had his way, she would live like this for the duration of her pregnancy and probably long after the baby came. He already wanted her to rest more, eat better and stress less. She knew if she didn't make these changes soon, he would push a little harder and he was not one to be denied.

She had yet to process what bringing a new life into their lives would mean. Obviously, she would have to put her daycare business on hold. That would be a huge adjustment for her and she wasn't sure how she felt about it. She loved what she did and the independence it provided her. Seeing to a baby, operating a business and not to mention, maintaining a marriage was a lot to deal with at one time. Faith realized something would have to give because she didn't see how she could do it all and do it all well. She acknowledged it was probably time to prepare the families she served to make other arrangements for childcare.

Just as her mind turned toward what happened the night before, Faith heard the garage door opening. She noticed it wasn't noon yet, so she wondered why Jamison was home so early. She smoothed the stray hair that had escaped her ponytail and looked down at the t-shirt and stretch pants she wore. It would have to do since she heard her husband already coming in the door.

She looked up and into the eyes of her lover, her friend, her man. She saw fatigue there. She also saw his apology. He didn't even have to say a word. She saw it.

"Hey," he said.

"Hey," she responded as she arose and moved toward him.

He opened his arms to receive her as she fell into her safe place and laid her face on his chest. She felt him kiss her on the head.

"I'm sorry," they said in concert, eliciting laughter from both of them.

Jamison pulled away to look into her eyes and said, "I was wrong for placing that demand on you. You're right. I do have to trust you and I do. But, I don't trust Evan. I'm sorry. It won't happen again."

"I thought about it and I would probably feel the same way. But, you have to trust me to do the right thing. I'm not trying to mess up what we have. Nothing and no one is worth it."

"I believe that. So, do you forgive me?"

"You know I do."

Faith and Jamison pecked each other on the lips a few times before their kisses deepened. Jamison pulled himself away from Faith long enough to ask, "Do you want to go upstairs? I need to show you just how sorry I am."

Faith took him by the hand and headed up the stairs. "Yes, I want to give you the opportunity to repent."

Chapter 13

Jamison pulled the car into the parking lot at Faith's obstetrician's office. He noticed someone waving. Once they got close, he realized it was Macie.

"What is Macie doing here?" Jamison wondered.

Faith dropped her head into her hand. "I told her I would just tell her about it when I got home. I guess that wasn't good enough."

Jamison got out of the car and went around to open Faith's door. He offered her his hand as she slid out of the vehicle.

"I know you're wondering why I'm here. Since I might not be here when the baby is born, I didn't want to miss today. At least I'll get to see him or her. Oh, will we find out whether it's a boy or girl today?"

Jamison frowned at Macie. "You weren't even supposed to be here, so you might not get to find out anything today."

Macie stopped and placed a hand on her hip. "Oh, you're not stopping me from seeing anything. I'll be right in there with y'all."

"Girl, you'll probably end up on the floor," Faith said, causing everyone to laugh.

They entered the office suite. Once Faith signed in, they were asked to take a seat in the waiting room.

"I hope they don't have us sitting here too long. They had me drinking water for this ultrasound and I need to go to the ladies room," Faith said, bouncing in her seat.

"I'll let them know." Macie approached the receptionist's desk. "Excuse me. Are you aware my friend is here for an ultrasound? She needs to be seen as soon as possible so she can go to the bathroom. Will she have to wait long?"

"Let me check." The receptionist looked at some file folders on the counter. "The tech should be with her shortly."

Macie returned to her seat to Faith and Jamison shaking their heads. "Why did you do that? Have some patience," Faith whispered.

The tech appeared in the door. "Mrs. Lewis?"

"Yes."

"You can come on back. I hope you weren't waiting too long with that full bladder. I don't know what happened. You should've been escorted right back."

Macie leaned over and said, "See."

Jamison helped Faith up as the trio prepared to go in for the ultrasound.

"Ma'am. Sir. I'm going to ask you to wait here while Mrs. Lewis is prepped. I'll call you back when she's ready."

"So, how well do you know Kardel? He seems like a nice guy." Macie raised her eyebrows up and down. "Is he dating anybody?"

"What difference does it make? You're moving to Atlanta soon."

"You might want to expand your business to Atlanta and he would be the perfect person to run it."

The tech appeared in the door again. "You two can come on back now."

When they arrived in the room, Faith was already lying on the bed with a drape over her bottom half. Jamison and Macie went to sit in the chair closest to Faith. Once Jamison shot her a look, Macie moved to the other seat. Faith chuckled and shook her head.

Once the technician began the ultrasound, the room was silent and all eyes were glued to the screen showing what was going on inside Faith's womb.

"Well, Mrs. Lewis. I think I know why you're a little larger than anticipated at this stage of your pregnancy."

"Why? Is everything okay?" Faith squinted as she viewed the screen.

"Everything's fine. You and Mr. Lewis are having triplets."

The realization of triplets took a few moments to register. A smile crept across Jamison's face.

"Did you say three babies?" Faith asked.

"Yes, ma'am. Let me show you." The tech moved the instrument around and pointed out the three small wonders growing inside of her.

Faith's hand flew to her mouth as tears came to her eyes. She turned her focus to Jamison. "Did you hear what she just said?"

"Yes, I did. I love you, baby." Jamison planted a sweet kiss on his wife's forehead. "I didn't think we could be any more blessed than we already are. Obviously, I was wrong."

Macie broke out dancing. "We're having triplets. We're having triplets," she sang. Laughter rang out in the room.

After the brief celebration, Jamison turned things back to a serious note. "Is there anything we need to be concerned about, since there are three babies?"

"I'm sure the doctor will go over all of that." She wiped the gel used for the ultrasound from Faith's belly with some paper towels. She helped Faith into a seated position with Jamison's help. Macie pulled her cell phone out and took an unexpected picture of Jamison and Faith.

"Why would you take a picture at this moment?" Faith asked.

"I'm going to post it to Facebook."

"Please don't. I'm in no condition to be seen on social media." Faith attempted to smooth her hair.

"Plus, I don't know if I want this information passed along to your Facebook followers," Jamison stated.

Macie looked from Faith to Jamison. "I forgot y'all are antisocial, but when those babies come, I'm going to make them Facebook famous. So, get ready."

Chapter 14

The music pumped as friends and family gathered in the Troy, Michigan, hotel ballroom for a gathering to wish Macie well on her new journey. Though it had taken a couple more months than expected, Macie finally received the job offer in Atlanta and accepted it. People were still flowing in, though the party had been in progress for almost two hours. Heavy hors d'oeuvres were spread on a number of tables around the room and champagne was being passed around on trays carried by the wait staff. The attendees filled the room with conversation and laughter.

Macie was dressed in a bright orange knee-length dress, making it difficult for her to be missed. She accented it with orange stilettos and a gold necklace with matching earrings and bracelet. As she mingled, she kept her eyes out for one special guest. After a few conversations, she spotted Faith speaking with Kardel, the person she'd been looking for. She moved through the crowd, hoping to reach them before someone else stopped her and she lost sight of them.

Faith noticed Macie approaching. "Hey, here's the woman of the hour." The two friends hugged.

Kardel smiled as he greeted Macie. "Hello, beautiful."

Macie returned the flirtation. "Hi, handsome." The two locked eyes, no longer noticing anyone else in the room.

"Um, if anyone cares," Faith said, looking from Macie to Kardel, "I think I'll go get off my feet for a few minutes." She smirked as she walked away from the couple who didn't seem to notice.

Jamison arrived at the table and followed his wife's gaze. "They're finally hooking up, huh?"

"It certainly appears so."

Jamison observed his wife. "How are you feeling? You okay?"

"Just a little tired," she said as she sighed.

"Maybe we should go."

"No, I can't leave in the middle of a party I threw."

"I don't care about this party." Jamison searched the room until he found Macie and Kardel, getting cozy on the dance floor. "I don't think Macie will miss you, anyway."

***

As the music changed from a fast song to a slow one, Kardel took Macie by the hand and pulled her toward him. As they rocked from side to side to the beat, Macie closed her eyes and allowed herself to relax. It seemed as though everything was perfect, except the timing. She wished they'd met each other earlier. At least that way, she wouldn't have to wonder what could have been once she moved to Georgia.

"I wish we had more time to get to know each other," Macie spoke.

"Yeah, I know."

Kardel pulled away, took her hands and continued to move side to side to the music.

"The attraction is undeniable. Don't you feel it?" Macie asked.

"Absolutely."

He pulled her back into him, all while keeping the beat.

The DJ went straight into another slow song.

"Let's go on a proper date before you leave and see what happens."

Macie looked up at Kardel. "Are you giving me a tryout?"

Kardel looked into her eyes. "No, I'm trying out. Maybe if I do well, you won't leave." He leaned down and planted a soft kiss on her lips.

A slow smile formed on Macie's face. "I'm going to enjoy you trying to convince me to stay." She lifted her head for another kiss and Kardel obliged.

***

A week later, Kardel held Macie's hand as they walked into the high-end seafood restaurant down the street from the theater. It would only be four more weeks before she moved to Georgia. As he opened the door for her, he affirmed his plan to spend as much time together as possible before she left.

The couple approached the hostess stand where Kardel referenced their reservation. Then, they were taken to their table.

Macie observed her surroundings. "Hmmm, nice restaurant." She nodded. "I didn't even know this was here."

"I have a few tricks up my sleeve."

Their waiter introduced himself, handed them menus, placed a basket of bread on the table, and took their drink orders. Once the waiter left, they perused their food options.

"Have you been here before?" Macie asked as she peeked at him over her menu.

"Yes, a few times." He folded his menu. "Is there a problem?"

"Everything is great. I was just going to ask you what you recommend."

Kardel recommended a few entrees. Shortly afterward, their waiter returned and they each placed their orders.

"So, how was your day?" Macie buttered a slice of bread and took a small bite.

"It was great. How was yours?"

"The same. I hung out with Faith a little earlier. I'm concerned about her."

"Yeah? What's going on?"

"I've never been pregnant, but this pregnancy seems to be wearing her out and she still has quite a bit of time to go. How is she going to make it until the end?"

"I would imagine it would be draining with three babies placing a demand on her body. Don't they give mothers prenatal vitamins for that?"

"They do." Macie looked away from her dinner companion. "I just hate I'm not going to be around to help out."

"She has Jamison."

"I know, but it's different. Faith and I are girls. We've always been there for each other and now she's getting ready for triplets and I'm going to be in Georgia."

Kardel reached for Macie's hand. "Are you second-guessing your decision to move?" He rubbed a thumb over her hand.

"You know, the timing couldn't be worse. I just met you and I want to spend more time together to see where things go. On top of that, Faith's pregnant. I'm wondering if I should be going or not." Macie released a sigh and looked off.

"Listen, Macie." Kardel leaned forward, maintaining physical contact. "I want to pursue a relationship with you, too. As far as Faith is concerned, if she needs additional support, you know Jamison will make sure she has it. If he feels like she needs you, he'll send for you. You know that man's love for his wife is without limits. She's going to be well taken care of. So, we've dealt with both of your concerns. If you want to take that opportunity, go and do it in peace."

Macie realized Kardel was right.

"You're right about Faith. Jamison will see to her needs." Macie shook her head slightly. "I can't explain it, but I feel like I might need to stick around."

"It's ultimately your decision and you won't get an argument from me if you decide to stay. Pray about it and see if you feel at peace. If you do, move to Georgia. If not, you know what to do."

Chapter 15

"What a way to celebrate our first anniversary, huh?"

"It's okay. We'll have plenty of anniversaries to celebrate. Besides, as long as I'm with you, it's a celebration."

"You are the most thoughtful man I know, and I'm so thankful to be your wife. A few days in Niagara Falls would've been awesome, but I'm glad you understand. Thank you, baby."

"You're welcome, honey. I told you, my job is to keep you happy. Now I know I'm doing a good job."

"Yes, you are. I love you."

"I love you more."

Faith and Jamison were relaxing in their master suite when the phone rang. Faith was recovering from a bout of morning sickness and Jamison was comforting her. He noted the number on the caller ID.

"It's my parents."

"Answer it. It might be important."

Jamison tapped the speaker phone button. "Hello."

"Hi, um, are you and Faith going to be home in about an hour? Your mother and I would like to come by."

"Hold on a minute. Let me see if Faith is feeling up to it." Jamison put the call on hold. "Do you feel up to a visit?" Faith sighed. "If not, just say so and I'll tell them this isn't a good time."

"It's okay. We need to talk."

"Are you sure?"

"Yes, I'm sure. Tell them to come on by."

An hour later, the doorbell rang and Jamison went to the door to answer it. His mother threw herself into his arms as his dad stood back and watched.

"I love you, no matter what. Don't ever forget that."

Jamison chuckled. "I love you too, Mom." Davore gave way for Hendrix to greet his son.

"Son, glad to see you." The men shook hands and Hendrix drew Jamison into a one-armed hug.

"Good to see you, too. Come on into the family room. Faith is resting there."

The family entered the family room, where Faith was sipping Vernors Ginger Ale and munching on saltine crackers.

Davore went to her. "Hi, dear. How are you feeling?" She reached out to hug her daughter-in-law.

"If I could keep food down, I wouldn't be half-bad." Faith and her mother-in-law shared a tense laugh.

"Yes, your grandbabies are giving her a hard time," Jamison commented.

Davore and Hendrix looked between Jamison and Faith. "Did you say grandbabies?"

"Oh, you two don't know. We're having triplets," Jamison said as he moved next to Faith.

"Oh, my goodness. You poor thing. I cannot imagine what that's like. Do triplets run in your family? They don't run in ours."

"Nobody in my family has had a multiple birth. I'll be the first."

"Hmm," Davore mumbled.

"This is certainly challenging," Faith said rubbing her belly, "but I wouldn't trade it for the world."

"Have a seat." Jamison gestured to the love seat as he sat on the sofa next to Faith.

Hendrix took a deep breath before speaking. "We came here to apologize for our behavior. We realize we were way out of line. The implication was unforgivable, but I hope you will forgive us," Hendrix directed his apology to Faith.

Faith nodded, before escaping to the bathroom.

Jamison shook his head and went behind her. "I hope this morning sickness subsides soon. I'll be right back."

Hendrix and Davore shook their heads. "Three children. What has our son gotten himself into?" Hendrix said.

Faith and Jamison returned moments later. Davore watched as Jamison held Faith with his arm around her on one side, holding her hand on the other.

"I'm sorry. Morning sickness, you know?"

"We understand," Hendrix said.

"I hope it goes away soon. I know it can be draining," Davore sympathized.

"Me too. I've actually lost a little weight."

"I think we should go so you can relax," Hendrix said as he stood, reaching to help Davore out of her seat.

"I wish you didn't have to rush off," Faith said.

"We'll check on you two again soon," Davore said, wrapping her arms around Faith, then Jamison.

Faith and Jamison saw the senior Lewises out of their home, just as another wave of nausea washed over Faith. She headed for the bathroom with Jamison following.

Chapter 16

Jamison and Faith entered the baby specialty store with one goal in mind...to begin the search for furniture for their babies' suite. Faith waddled through the store looking for the baby furniture section, stopping to look at dresses for baby girls, suits with bowties for boys and other things that caught her eye. Soon, she found herself with several items in her hand.

"Honey, would you mind getting a basket for this stuff?" Faith waved the items for Jamison to see.

"Baby, I know the ultrasound showed we're having two girls and a boy. What if they're wrong? I told you what happened to my friend and his wife."

"We can always bring things back if they don't work out. Everything is just so cute, it's hard for me to resist."

"I thought we agreed we were shopping for cribs today. People will bring a lot of this stuff to the shower."

"But—"

Jamison interrupted, "When the babies are born, we will come out here and buy all the cute little clothes you want. Okay?" He took the items from her hands and hung them up.

Faith's shoulders slumped, but she acquiesced and headed toward the furniture department. When they arrived, they found about twenty different collections, each available in multiple finishes. The salesperson in that area informed them there were many more online as well. Faith realized this was going to take a while. She hadn't even considered dressers and chests for the children's room.

Faith stood with her arms spread out to her sides. "Where should we start? Do you see anything you like?"

Faith followed Jamison's gaze to a weathered taupe wood set, with an attached changing table and a bank of drawers. She walked toward the set with him close behind. The furniture was sophisticated and upscale. It was also convenient since the bed could convert to a toddler bed and eventually a full size bed as the children grew. The matching storage pieces looked good as well.

"I love this and I know you do," Faith said.

Jamison rubbed his hand over the crib as if memorizing every angle. He stood there studying the furniture for several moments. Faith thought he'd forgotten about her presence.

"Hello," she said, waving her hands over her head.

Finally, he looked up at her. "Do you realize we have three extensions of our love coming in a very short period of time? They're going to be completely dependent on us for everything. We're going to be responsible for their upbringing. It just dawned on me how heavy that is."

"I know better than you." She patted her growing middle and chuckled. "I'm supplying temporary housing for them."

"Yeah, that's true. You and our children won't ever have to worry about anything. I'll always be there. Whatever I have to do to take care of you, I'll do it. Trust me."

Faith leaned into him and he pulled her close. "You make me feel so safe and loved. I know I never have to worry about being taken care of." They stood for a time. "So, is this the set?"

"I think so. Now, the next question is how many dressers we'll need to hold all of those clothes you want to buy."

Faith began counting on her fingers. "We might need to knock a wall or two down to hold it all, but we'll do what we need to do."

Chapter 17

"I know you're intent on going to this event tonight, so I'm not going to say what I really want to say." Jamison's voice boomed in Faith's vehicle's phone system.

"Everything will be fine. It's a simple dance recital." Faith shook her head. "I don't know what you're so worried about."

"I told you I don't trust Evan and I really don't want you around him. I would feel better if I went with you, but I have an important meeting this evening. I think Kardel is even gone."

"Kardel has plans with Macie. Besides, he's been covering for you quite a bit here lately. Don't want to wear him out before the babies come."

"You might have a point there. Call me the minute it's over, so I'll know when you're on your way home."

"I will, I promise. I'm pulling into the parking lot now. I'll talk to you in an hour or two."

"All right, baby. I love you."

"I love you, too." Faith disconnected the phone call. A pain ran through her belly. Before she had time to touch it, it stopped. "I wonder what that was."

Faith entered the dance center and encountered the crowd of faces belonging to the children's parents, grandparents and family friends. She followed the crowd, figuring they would lead her to the location of the recital.

"Faith," she heard a familiar voice calling to her from somewhere in the crowd. Her reflex was to look for where it came from. Someone touched her on the arm and she turned to find Evan standing a little behind her to her left.

"Hi, Evan." Faith looked away from him. The awkwardness between them was palpable.

Evan reached over to hug her and she responded by reaching back.

Evan stepped back after noticing her baby bump. "Whoa! Look at you."

"Yes, we're expecting. Actually, we have triplets on the way."

"Triplets. Wow. I guess things are working out well for you and Jamison."

"Yes, it's great. So, congratulations to you and Janay."

"For what?"

"You two getting back together and the pregnancy."

"What pregnancy?"

"I saw Janay in the drug store buying a pregnancy test."

"She's not pregnant and we're not exactly together. We're separated."

"Oh, I'm sorry. I just assumed based on the test..."

"It's okay. We haven't given up completely."

"Oh, well, I guess I'd better go find a seat," Faith said as she headed in the direction of the theater.

"No, you have to see the Ns. They're with Janay. They should be here any second." He looked at his watch.

"I guess I should. I haven't seen them in quite a while."

The two stood in the middle of the hallway as people traveled on either side of them. The awkward silence between them was swallowed up by the voices of the other people in attendance.

"Do you need to sit?" Evan asked, reaching for Faith's elbow.

"I think so."

"There's a bench right over here." Evan and Faith sat on the bench as another pain traveled across Faith's abdomen.

***

Janay and the Ns walked into the dance center and looked for Evan. Since she arrived later than expected, there wasn't time to hunt him down visually. She pulled her cell phone out of her purse to text him. Before she had the chance, Nia spotted him.

"There he is!" she yelled as she took off running with Nahla following. Janay went behind them, holding Naomi by the hand.

She saw her daughters hugging their father, then the person sitting next to him. She squinted to identify the woman with Evan. Nahla and Nia seemed familiar enough with her to hug her.

When she arrived where the group gathered, she looked at the woman and sucked her teeth.

"What are you doing here?" she asked as Naomi reached for Faith. Janay refused to release her youngest child and the toddler began to cry.

"Nia and Nahla invited me to come see them dance. Is there going to be a problem?"

Janay noticed Nia and Nahla clinging to Faith and felt a familiar negative emotion rise up within her. She didn't want to upset her daughters by sending Faith away. The connection between their former babysitter and her children needed to be broken. It was simply unacceptable to her. She would address this issue with Evan later.

"Great. We can be one big make-believe family." She gave Naomi to Evan, though the girl was still reaching for Faith. "I need to take Nia and Nahla to get changed, then I need to make sure they're where they need to be. I'll find you afterward." She left in search of Nia and Nahla's dance teams.

***

"I guess we should go into the recital hall," Evan said as he led Naomi and Faith through the corridor.

"Really, I think I should sit separately. I don't want there to be any problems with Janay."

"We'll be okay. Trust me." Evan found a row of seats near the top of the hall. He led Naomi down a few steps then, he reached back and helped Faith.

Once they were seated, Naomi finally succeeded in getting to Faith. She held Faith's face in her little hands and planted kisses all over her face.

Janay found the trio and sat on the other side of Evan. She couldn't stand Faith. Her counselor had repeatedly told her forgiveness was crucial for her recovery. However, this woman required a whole different level of forgiveness Janay wasn't capable of just yet.

Faith's eyes met Janay's as Naomi snuggled her head under Faith's chin. Janay watched as Evan rubbed the side of their youngest daughter's face. She found herself jealous. Once again, Faith had weaseled herself right back into their lives and Janay wasn't going to rest until she was out again, for good this time.

The recital started and everyone's attention turned toward the stage. Thirty minutes into the performances, Nia and Nahla bounced onto the stage with the rest of their ballet class. Each girl in the class had their hair pulled up into a bun or away from their face with a headband. The white leotards, pink tutus, white tights and ballet shoes was the uniform for this performance. The performance went well and the group received a standing ovation. Nahla looked into the crowd until her eyes fell on their row. She blew a kiss to them, drawing a response from each of them in kind. She took a deep bow, causing them all to laugh.

Janay gave Faith the side eye, only to notice her eyes were large and the woman was bent over, clutching her abdomen. A groan escaped Faith's mouth. Janay tapped Evan on the shoulder and pointed at the woman. Evan turned his complete attention to Faith, much to Janay's chagrin. Janay noticed a trickle of blood run down the leg belonging to her nemesis.

"I think she might be miscarrying, Evan. You'd better call her husband and 911. I have to go get Nia and Nahla. Give me Naomi. I'll take her with me."

***

Faith overheard the comment Janay made and noticed the blood streaming down her leg as well. The pain she'd felt earlier returned and lingered longer this time.

She looked up at Evan. "I can't lose my babies. I just can't."

"I'm calling 911. Then, I'll call Jamison for you. Try to say calm."

Faith's leg began to bounce on its own. She was glad Evan was taking care of these phone calls, even though she preferred to speak to Jamison herself. After the EMTs were contacted, he called Jamison.

"Jamison, listen, I had to call 911 for Faith. She's in some pain. As soon as they get here, I'll ride over with her in the ambulance." He was quiet as Jamison spoke. "There's no need for violence, man. I didn't do anything to her. She was just sitting here and after the Ns got done, Janay noticed she was bleeding a little." He was quiet for a few more seconds. "Here's Faith."

"I don't know what's going on. Janay said I might be having a miscarriage, but I don't know. Okay, honey. I'll see you at St. Joe's."

The emergency technicians arrived and took Faith's vital signs. Janay returned with the Ns in time to see Faith being placed on the gurney. Nahla escaped her mother's grasp and approached her former babysitter.

"What's wrong, Miss Faith?" she asked as tears flooded her face.

"Don't worry, honey. Everything's all right. I'll talk to you soon. Okay?" Faith finished her sentence as she was being rolled out of the theater.

Evan looked at Janay. "I don't want her to go over there by herself, so I'm going with her. Jamison is on his way."

Janay grabbed her estranged husband by the arm. "She doesn't need you. She's got a husband. Besides, this is your night with the Ns."

Evan pulled away from her. "I know Faith's a married woman, but I think it's the right thing to do, unless you want to go with her." He ran to catch the gurney.

Janay didn't even respond to Evan's ridiculous statement. It seemed she'd lost to Faith again. She looked down at her daughters and drew them close.

"Tomorrow's a school day, so we have to get baths and lay clothing out."

"But, we're supposed to go to Daddy's house tonight," Nia pointed out.

"I know, but Daddy went to help Miss Faith. You can go to his house tomorrow night."

"Can we go see about Miss Faith? I'm really worried about her," Nahla wondered aloud.

"The hospital will take great care of her, so don't you worry."

As Janay directed the car toward Big Momma's house, she wondered if Evan would ever be ready to resume their normal marriage relationship. The way he stepped up to help Faith concerned her. He was too willing to abandon his family to aid Faith and that just didn't seem right.

Chapter 18

Jamison punched the elevator call button several times, but it wasn't coming fast enough. He ran to the door leading to the staircase and leapt down the stairs a flight at a time. He pushed the door at the bottom open, causing it to hit the wall behind it with such force, it left a dent. He sprinted to his car and waited until it recognized the key fob in his pocket that would allow him to enter.

Speeding toward Interstate 75, Jamison accessed his car's phone system to call his parents and Macie, who was with Kardel. He told them what was going on with Faith and they all headed for the hospital as well.

Jamison wondered what happened at the recital that caused this to happen. Did the stress of dealing with the Ingrams cause a problem for her? Did Evan or Janay do something to her? Did she have to walk too far to get into the building? Did someone bump her and put the babies at risk? All of these possibilities swirled in his mind as he weaved in and out of traffic to get to his family.

While he didn't know what was going on medically, he knew that if Evan was responsible, he would deal with him man-to-man. Maybe the man didn't know he lost. Perhaps, he couldn't accept it. After this, Jamison promised himself he would make sure Evan knew Faith was his wife and Evan's family needed to move on with that understanding. It was time for the Ingrams to disconnect, so she could focus on their new family.

Taking care of three newborns at once was going to take up most, if not all of her time. He wasn't interested in hurting the Ns feelings and he truly understood their connection to Faith. However, it wasn't his job to figure out how to explain that Faith moved on with her life and they couldn't be with her like they used to. It was Janay and Evan's job to do this in a way that wouldn't damage the children. He had a feeling Evan was allowing the children to stay connected, since it also allowed him access.

His phone rang, but his vehicle's Bluetooth function didn't answer the call. He picked up his phone and noticed Faith's number on the display. He fumbled with it but managed to keep it from falling. He pressed the answer button. He looked up as he said, "Hello," and saw brake lights. He slammed on his brakes, but ran into the back of an eighteen-wheeler in front of him.

***

Evan dropped the phone. After Jamison answered his phone, Evan heard what sounded like brakes screeching and a vehicle crash. The call hadn't disconnected, so he retrieved and placed it to his ear. Nothing.

"Jamison? Are you there?"

No response.

Unsure of what to do, he disconnected the call and paced the Labor and Delivery waiting room. A few moments later, Macie ran in with a man he didn't know.

She ran past him without acknowledging his presence and straight to the nurse's station.

"I'm looking for my friend, Faith Lewis. Can you tell me where she is?"

The nurse punched some information into the system. "Ma'am, the doctor is still examining her. When she knows more, she'll come out and share it with you."

Macie noticed Evan. "What are you doing here?"

"I was with her when this happened."

Macie scowled. "I'm confused. Why were the two of you together in the first place?"

"She was at the Ns' dance recital when this whole thing happened. I didn't want her to be by herself."

"Well, you can leave now," she said, dismissing him.

"Not until I hear what the doctor says."

Macie returned her attention to him. "Are you kidding me? If I were you, I would leave before Jamison gets here. He'll probably blame you for Faith's condition."

Hearing Jamison's name reminded Evan about the phone call. "I called Jamison to let him know we were at the hospital and it sounded like he had a car accident. I called his name a few times after that, but he didn't answer." Evan handed Faith's cell phone to Macie.

"I'll call him and see if I can find out what's going on." Kardel headed to the hall to make the call.

In the meantime, Jamison's parents rushed into the room. "What's going on?" Davore asked Macie looking around the room. "Jamison hasn't made it here yet?"

"Evan was on the phone with Jamison when he was on the way over here. He thinks he had a car accident. Kardel is trying to get in touch with him now."

"Faith's old boyfriend, Evan?" Hendrix asked.

"Yes, he's right over there." Macie pointed at Evan. "Hendrix and Davore, this is Evan. These are Jamison's parents."

Evan waved while Hendrix and Davore glared at him.

Kardel returned to the room and said, "He didn't answer, but someone else at the scene heard the phone ringing and answered it. There was a bad car accident. Apparently, Jamison ran into the back of a truck."

"Dear God," Hendrix lamented.

Davore looked at Evan, who backed away. She stalked toward him. "I knew you were still involved with Faith. You shouldn't even be here," she screamed, before burying her face into her husband's chest.

"I think you should leave, Evan," Kardel said.

"Lewis family?" a doctor called out from the hall. "Is the Lewis family here?"

The group stampeded the doctor to hear what she had to say.

101

"We're the Lewises. How's Faith?" Davore inquired.

The doctor looked down at a file. "Faith is fine. The triplets are a different story."

"Doctor, please tell us what's going on," Davore said.

"Her water broke and we're concerned about one of the babies so we're going to deliver them."

Macie stepped forward and asked, "Isn't it too early for the babies to be born? She's only six or seven months along."

"Pregnancies involving multiples often don't go the full forty weeks, like single pregnancies do. We have a whole unit dedicated to babies who are born early, so we're prepared to provide the care they'll need. We want to make sure we're doing the right thing for the babies as well as Mrs. Lewis."

"So, they'll be okay?" Davore asked.

"We're going to do our best, but preemies often face some challenges." She looked among the faces of the Lewis family. "Are there any more questions?"

"When can we see her?" Macie asked.

"Mr. Lewis, your wife's been asking for you. If you'll follow me, I'll take you to her," the doctor said to Evan."

"This is not her husband. My son is and he's not here yet. We're hoping he'll be here shortly." Davore looked at Macie. "I think you should go back and be with her."

"What am I going to tell her when she asks about Jamison?"

Davore tapped her chin with her forefinger. "Tell her he's not here yet. It's the truth. We don't want to upset her with news of the accident."

"Maybe you should go too, honey. Kardel and I are going to check on Jamison," Hendrix said, glancing at Kardel who nodded in agreement.

"I think it's best I stay out here." Davore stole a glance at Evan.

"Suit yourself." Macie followed the doctor. She glanced over her shoulder. "Kardel, text me when you get more information about Jamison."

"You got it."

The two men left the room, leaving Davore and Evan glaring at each other. She rolled her eyes at him and took a seat.

Evan looked through the glass separating the waiting room and the hallway leading to where Faith was.

"Don't even think about it," Davore said.

Evan pushed his hands into his pockets and stood there briefly before leaving the room.

***

Macie saw the doctor stop and point to a room about three-quarters of the way down the hall. When she reached it, she said to Macie, "I'll be back shortly." She nodded her head and entered.

Right away, Macie noticed the fatigue in Faith's eyes. "Hey, girl. I know you like attention, but you didn't have to get it this way." The duo laughed. Macie was happy to see her friend smile.

ing to change my plans and sticking around here if I can."

"I get the feeling the triplets aren't the only reason you're thinking about staying."

"Kardel is a consideration. I tried to talk your husband into starting an Atlanta division of the agency so Kardel could move too, but I don't think I convinced him."

"That doesn't surprise me. Those two have been friends for a long time. I don't think they could bear being apart from each other."

"You're probably right."

"I wish my husband would get here. I know he would hate to miss the birth of these children."

"I'm sure he'll be here any minute."

"Something doesn't feel right, though. I hope everything is okay."

Macie felt a phone vibrate in her purse. When she realized it was Faith's phone, she said, "I'll be right back," and stepped into the hall. She looked at the phone's screen which read, "ICE Jamison."

She answered the phone and spoke to a police officer at the scene of Jamison's accident. Her breath caught in her throat when she heard what he said. She started toward the room and stopped herself before re-entering. She couldn't go back in there right now. Instead, she decided to contact the others to share this new information.

***

"Let's stop in the emergency room and see if he's here yet." Hendrix and Kardel rushed through the hospital in search of Jamison.

They found the ER and went to the counter. "Do you have a Jamison Lewis here?"

The nurse looked up at him. "Sir, privacy laws prohibit me from giving you that information."

"He's my son and he was in a car accident. We think he'll be brought here."

The receptionist keyed in some information and waited to see what came up. "Sir, he's not here."

"Thank you," Hendrix said. "That's helpful." He turned toward Kardel. "I guess we need to head over to the scene."

"If we do that, we might miss him. I think we should just stay here."

Hendrix paced the floor. "Maybe we should call the police and see if we can find out something."

Kardel's phone rang and when he looked at it, it was Macie. "Hey. Are you crying? Is everything okay?"

"No, it's not okay. Where are you? Are you still at the hospital?"

"We haven't left the hospital yet. We're in ER. Should we come back up there?"

"No. I'm coming down there."

Minutes later, Macie appeared in the emergency room and threw herself into Kardel's welcoming arms. "What's going on? Is it Faith? My God, is it the babies?"

Macie frantically looked around. "Where's Davore?"

"We thought she was in the waiting room."

"We need to find her. You might want to call her," Macie said to Hendrix.

"Macie, calm down. What is going on?"

Macie gathered herself before she spoke. She looked at the two men standing beside her. "It's Jamison. He didn't survive the accident. He's gone."

***

Davore ran through the hospital corridors, looking for Evan. She finally found him a ways down the hall and she sped up as he turned a corner. She saw him getting on an elevator. The doors were closing as she approached so she stuck her foot in their path. The doors opened allowing Davore access to the space.

"Evan, before you go, can I talk to you for a moment?"

"I don't think so."

"Please," Davore begged.

Evan excused himself from the elevator. "What do you want?"

"I just have a few questions about you and Faith."

"That was a while ago and we both moved on. I don't owe anyone an explanation."

"You've both moved on, yet you're here."

Evan paused. "Yes, I'm here. There's no law against it."

"You're in love with her. I can tell."

Evan remained silent.

"I'll get right to the point. When was the last time you two were together?"

"Together?"

"Don't act like you don't know what I'm asking. When?"

"Not that it's your business, but, never."

"I don't believe that for one minute." Davore grabbed his arm.

Evan looked at her hand on his arm. "Would you mind taking your hand off me?"

"Um-hmm." Davore turned to walk away, but spun back around. "Just one more thing."

"What's that?"

"Could the triplets be yours?"

Evan's mouth dropped, then he shook his head. "There is no way Faith's children are mine." He walked around Davore and punched the button for the elevator a few times.

"Tell me. It's going to come out one day anyway. I'll see to it."

When the elevator doors opened, Hendrix, Macie and Kardel appeared.

"Did you find Jamison?" Davore asked. The trio looked from one to another. "What did you find out? Where is he? Is he in the emergency room?"

Hendrix took his wife by the shoulders. His tears flowed as he said, "Jamison passed away, honey." Davore didn't respond. "Davore, did you hear me?"

Suddenly, a smile spread across Davore's face. "This is no time to joke, Hendrix. Where's Jamison?" she asked, as she playfully swatted Hendrix's arm. Davore looked around and noticed no one else was smiling.

"Sweetheart, I wish I was playing around, but I'm not. Our son passed away."

"What do you mean, he passed away?"

Hendrix lifted his head as tears continued their trek down his chin to his neck. "He died, honey. He's gone."

Several emotions transitioned across Davore's face before a screech escaped her mouth and her body crumbled to the floor. Hendrix and Kardel picked her up. Hendrix steadied her as she released her tears onto his chest.

"We need to get back to the waiting room in case the doctor has more news on Faith."

Davore stumbled as the group moved to the waiting room. She turned to see Evan hadn't moved. "Mark my words," she yelled, "you're going to pay for this!"

Chapter 19

Evan called Janay after leaving the hospital. Hearing about Jamison's death felt like a punch to his gut. He couldn't imagine how Faith must feel. Though he and Jamison could no longer be considered friends, there was a time when the two men got along great. He admired Jamison as a man and businessman, despite the fact their mutual respect had been impacted by Evan's feelings for Faith. Regardless of any of that, he hated to hear the man had passed away.

"Hello, Evan. What do you want?" Janay's attitude was obvious from her greeting.

"Um, I was calling to see if the girls were still up."

"They're just about to go to bed. Why?"

"Since it's my parenting time, I wanted to pick them up if that's okay with you."

"When I left you at the dance school, you were too busy taking care of Faith to be concerned about your parenting time. What changed?"

"Can I come pick them up? Please, Janay. Don't give me a hard time."

"Why can't you just get them tomorrow night?"

Evan paused as tears welled up in his eyes. "Tomorrow isn't promised."

Janay didn't respond immediately. "Are you crying? What happened at that hospital tonight?"

Evan gathered himself enough to answer. "I was talking to Jamison on the phone, trying to let him know what was going on with Faith when he had a car accident. He died, baby. Right there on the phone with me." Evan's emotions spilled over.

Janay took a deep breath. "Wow. I did not expect to hear that. How is Faith?"

"I don't know. Once they took her back, I didn't see her again. I wanted to check on her, but her mother-in-law wouldn't allow it."

"Oh, you're not upset about Jamison. You're really upset because you don't know what's happening with Faith."

"Look, I know you're still angry and you may still need some time to work through everything, but I've been thinking since I left the hospital. I want you and the girls to come home. If we're going to work this out, we need to do it in the same house."

"You're just feeling emotional because of what happened to Jamison. You might feel differently in a week or two."

"That's not true. What it did was make me realize how temporary life is and while we're going back and forth about who

111

did what and why, we're missing out on time we could be together."

"I don't know, Evan. I think you still have feelings for Faith and I can't handle that."

"I'll probably always care about her, but she's someone else's wife. She's no longer available to me."

"You just told me Jamison passed away. She's very available."

"I love you. I have since the day I saw you in the hallway in high school. I made a mistake. Actually, we both made mistakes. But, that's all over now. I don't want something to happen and we haven't given our marriage everything we've got. Please give us another chance."

"We'll come for tonight. We'll see how it goes after that."

"I'll take that. See you in a few."

Evan was ecstatic about the potential for a new start with Janay. He knew they would have to take things slow, but he was more committed than ever to make things work. Whatever he had to do, he would.

His mind switched to thoughts of Faith. The look on her face when she started feeling pain and saw blood trickling down her legs was still stuck in his head. To think about what Jamison's death would do to her was beyond his own comprehension. He was certain she would be devastated and he wanted to be a friend and support for her if he was allowed. However, he'd just promised Janay he was no longer interested in Faith in that way. Would Janay trust him being there for Faith in a purely platonic way?

Chapter 20

The staff was moving Faith down the hospital corridors into the operating room to prepare her for the Cesarean section she needed in order to give birth. She felt the effects of the medication they'd given her to deaden the area where the incision would be made. She felt her body shake from anxiety. She looked over at Macie and noted the concern on her face. In fact, her in-laws and Kardel seemed a little somber when she'd seen them. And, where was Jamison? She still didn't have the answer to that question. She decided she couldn't worry about that right now, because it was time to bring the triplets into the world. She would deal with Jamison about his absence later.

"Are you sure you want to do this, Macie? You can turn back if you want to. I won't be mad at you. Truthfully, if I didn't have to go, I wouldn't."

"Are you kidding me? I wouldn't miss it for anything in the world." She gave Faith a stiff smile.

Faith's eyebrows went up. "All right. What is going on? Why does it seem like you and everybody else knows something I don't know?"

"Girl, that must be the drugs they gave you making you paranoid. Now, you need to focus on the task at hand and that's delivering these babies, so Aunt Macie can begin spoiling them."

"If you're going to be the one taking care of them, then go right ahead and spoil them."

The team slowed the gurney down as they waited for the doors to open, taking them closer to the operating room. Faith tried to calm herself. In just a few moments, she and Jamison would become parents.

They finally brought the gurney to a stop under several bright lights. Three small bassinets were in position, surrounded by numerous items needed to tend to their needs when they were born. Faith exhaled a breath she wasn't aware she was holding as they placed a sheet at her chest level to block her view of the surgical site.

Macie reappeared at her side and smiled at her again. "Here we go," she said. "Let's make you a mommy."

***

Faith smiled as she thought about the boy and two girls she'd just given birth to. Tears sprang to her eyes as she marveled at the miracle that was their birth. Though they were tiny because of their prematurity, she could see they were the perfect blend of Jamison and her. She looked around the room and noted Jamison's continued absence.

"Has anyone heard from Jamison?" She looked at her in-laws, Macie and Kardel as they glanced at each other.

Kardel stepped forward. "They let us see the babies and they, um, are beautiful." Faith noted his uneasiness. Her in-laws' heads were down, while Macie looked out of the window.

Faith tried to sit up but was instantly reminded of the incision across her belly. "I know something is going on with Jamison, because there's no way he would've missed this. Will someone please tell me?"

Davore opened her mouth to speak, but was interrupted when Hendrix spoke. "Honey, I'll tell her." He pulled a chair up next to the bed and took Faith's hand.

Faith felt her heart sink. "Wait. Where is he? Is he okay?" She glanced at those in the room, then let her gaze fall on her father-in-law.

"There was a car accident while he was driving over here." Faith's free hand flew to her mouth and sobs began to escape her lips.

"Oh, my God. Don't tell me…"

"Faith, he didn't make it."

Faith squeezed the pillow placed over her belly. She bent over and released a guttural scream. Davore, Macie and Kardel rushed to her side. She was crying so hard, she couldn't catch her breath. Macie pressed the call button, summoning the nursing staff who responded immediately.

"Mrs. Lewis, you have to calm down. Take some deep breaths." Faith didn't respond.

"What brought this on?" the nurse asked, directing her question to Macie.

"Her husband passed away," Macie responded.

"It may not have been the best decision to tell her right now."

"She kept asking for him. We had to tell her," Macie explained.

"What's done is done. I'll call her doctor."

The group covered her in hugs and comforting words. The nurse returned and inserted the needle into Faith's IV, causing the woman to relax. The group allowed her to lay back in the bed and rest.

***

The next day, Faith made her way to the NICU where her children Mercy, Grace and Jamison Jr. were being cared for. She scanned her wristband, allowing her entry into the unit. The nurses directed her to the children belonging to her and Jamison. Jamison. Her now late-husband.

As she viewed the babies, a fresh wave of grief washed over her. Thoughts of raising these little people, especially Jamison Jr., caused her concern. He would need a strong male influence in his life, being a boy in a house full of women. But, she couldn't really deal with that at the moment. She had more pressing issues to tend to.

She waved the nurse over to get an update. "Can I help you, Mrs. Lewis?"

"Yes, I was just wondering how my babies are doing. They're so little."

"They're doing well. By the way, I wanted to express my condolences for the death of your husband. I know it must be tough, but we'll take good care of your son and daughters until they're ready to come home. Don't worry about them."

"It wasn't supposed to be like this. We were supposed to raise them together. Now, I've got to do it alone."

"You must be able to handle it. Otherwise, God wouldn't have brought you to this place." Faith glanced at the woman. "I'm sorry if I spoke out of turn. It just sort of slipped out." Faith turned her attention back to her daughter. "Is there anything else I can do for you, Mrs. Lewis?"

"No, I think that's it. I heard I might be going home today, so I thought I should check on them before I leave. Thank you so much for caring for them."

"You're welcome, Mrs. Lewis. It's my job and my honor to do so. I promise you, everything is going to work out just fine for you and these precious babies. If you need anything else, just let me know." The nurse went to the other side of the unit.

Faith pulled up a chair to the group of bassinets and looked between the three children.

"Hi, this is your mommy. I love you. I can't wait for you to come home, but you're too tiny right now." Tears trickled down her cheeks. "I don't know what's going to happen, but I promise I'm going to do all I can to raise you to be the best you can be. Your father loved you so much. I'm sorry you won't ever get a chance to meet him. He was a wonderful man and I'm going to make sure you know all about him. I'm going back to my room so I can get some rest. I'll see you again soon."

Chapter 21

The custom black casket positioned at the end of the aisle made the reality of Jamison's death real for Faith. Seeing the side of the face she fell in love with caused her knees to weaken. If she wasn't flanked by her father and Kardel, she was certain she would have fallen to the floor.

She thought about the three babies who were in the hospital's neonatal intensive care unit. Though they were born early, they were improving faster than the doctors expected. Faith wasn't surprised by that. These were Jamison's children. They were warriors.

She approached what remained of her husband. She shook loose from those that supported her so she could have this sacred moment alone with the man who had stolen her heart. She loved him so much and still hadn't been able to wrap her mind around the fact this would be the last time she would see him on this side of Heaven. She ran her hand over his head, shocked by the coldness of his skin where she was accustomed to warmth. She viewed the black velvet suit coat he wore with the gray and white brocade vest over a crisp white shirt. She leaned over and kissed his lips, allowing them to linger there, though he couldn't respond. The tears flowed, falling on his face.

Her father touched her on the shoulder. "Faith," he said. She knew what he was trying to tell her, but she couldn't comply with his request. She couldn't bring herself to walk away. To do so would mean this was real. This was happening. She wondered how she would ever live without this man when he was her life. Faith had never understood people wanting to get into the casket with their loved ones, until this very moment. She wanted to go with Jamison wherever he went. Kardel appeared on her other side. He and her father attempted to move her toward the seat reserved for her, the widow, and she allowed them to move her back a step.

"No," she barked, shaking them off again.

Faith's mother came to her side. "Honey, you'll always have him in your heart."

"I know he's in my heart, but I want him here with me!" Faith yelled at her mother. "Don't you understand? I'll sit when I'm ready." Faith's mother stood back and allowed her daughter to continue her vigil.

The funeral directors came forward. One of them whispered to Faith, "Mrs. Lewis, you'll have more time with your husband. Right now, all of these people want to support you. Let them." Faith looked over her shoulder at the people gathered there. They were there because they loved and respected Jamison and wanted to show it by helping her through this nightmare. She acquiesced and allowed herself to be helped to her seat.

After Faith was seated, Jamison's parents spent a few moments with their son. Kardel said goodbye to his dear friend, followed by other family, friends and strangers who paid their final respects.

Faith's mother handed her a handkerchief and gave her a supportive smile. People began to flow past her in a blur as her hand was shaken, she was hugged, and people told her what a wonderful man her husband was and how sorry they were about what happened.

She heard a familiar voice and looked up to find Evan. "I'm so sorry for your loss, Faith. If there's anything I can do, don't hesitate to let me know." Faith stood and hugged him. Tight. She needed to feel the comfort of the arms of a man she knew cared for her. Though she wasn't sure how he felt about her now, she knew he once cared for her and that was enough. She wasn't sure if or when she would experience this again, so she savored it for as long as possible. She released him and looked into his eyes. She saw shock and surprise.

Hendrix launched out of his seat and appeared beside her. "Show some respect. How could you do this on the day we bury my son?"

Faith was amazed at how Hendrix seemed to overlook the fact that it wasn't just their son, but her husband and her children's father, who was laying in that casket. Instead of voicing her feelings, Faith decided to take a seat in order to avoid making a scene. Hendrix returned to his seat next to Davore, who rolled her eyes at her daughter-in-law.

The moment came when the funeral directors were set to close the casket. This was her final chance to see him, touch him and tell him goodbye. She took Kardel's hand as he led her there. A fresh flow of tears appeared as she realized though she wanted to, she couldn't stand in this place forever. She touched Jamison's hand and whispered words of love, respect and devotion. Though she knew he couldn't hear her, it was helpful for her to say them. Then, she stepped away for the final time.

As the casket was closing, a woman walked up the aisle. "Wait," she said. "Please, I need to see him one last time."

One of the funeral home employees walked over to Faith. "Do you give us permission to reopen the casket?"

Faith looked at the unfamiliar woman. The gaze the woman returned seemed to dare Faith to deny her request.

"No. We need to move on." She took her seat.

"Who's that?" Vonda asked her daughter.

"I have no idea and I don't have the energy to find out."

When the pastor asked for people to come forth and give words, Faith made the decision on the spur of the moment to speak. She stood next to the casket and began to speak.

"This was totally unplanned, but I just felt in my heart I needed to say a few words about this great man. What made this man great is not The Lewis Agency, the home we live in or any of the trappings our lifestyle affords us. What made him great is the love and care he extended to all of you. What made him great is the pro bono work he did every day for people who needed his services but couldn't afford it. What made him great was the way he cherished, loved, respected and cared for his family, even our children he never got to see. You are looking at a woman who is well-loved. Jamison and I are true soulmates," she said as she laid her hand on the casket. "I love you, Jamison. Not just today, but forever."

Chapter 22

Faith opened her eyes to clanking pots and pans as well as the smell of bacon. She felt her stomach turn. She turned over, looking at Jamison's side of the bed. He was still gone. She wasn't dreaming nor was she in a coma. This was reality.

The vision of her husband laying in that casket would probably never leave. As tears made their way down her cheeks, she wondered if she would ever run out of them. Soon, the sobs she'd been holding in escaped as well. Life would never be the same.

Now, with three little ones, she had to figure out how to handle the deep sadness she'd felt since the moment she'd heard Jamison passed away. It had deepened once she realized the battle her children would have to fight. Sure, she'd been successful convincing everyone she was okay, but she was just about out of the strength required to keep that charade going.

Truthfully, Faith felt like she wouldn't be able to continue on. How would she ever get over losing Jamison, taking care of three preemies, and living her life? She was exhausted physically, spiritually and emotionally, and her new reality had just begun.

Her body was sore from the Caesarian section. Her heart ached because of her loss.

She sat up slowly, hugging her midsection, and placed her feet in the slippers situated on the floor by the bed. Slippers Jamison purchased for her just a couple of months ago. She reached for the robe laying at the foot of the bed. As she stood, she slipped it over her body and went to the bathroom. As she washed her hands, she stole a glance at herself in the mirror. It seemed she'd aged just since the night before. There was no trace of the joy that was resident there just four weeks ago.

Jamison's vanity came into view in the mirror. She turned and stood in front of it. All of his personal belongings were still there. His electric razor, his toothbrush, his hair brush, and mouthwash were still sitting there. She moved to the closet and fingered the numerous suits, shirts, pants, and sport coats. Pulling a shirt to her face, she inhaled his scent. It comforted her. The labeled boxes containing Jamison's huge shoe collection caught her attention. A weak smile crossed her face as she thought about his love for shoes. What was she supposed to do with all of this stuff? Everything that was Jamison's needed to be dealt with in some way. But how?

"Your father wanted to take care of those things for you." Faith looked up to see her mother leaning against the door frame with her arms crossed. "I told him not to take you too fast."

She ran her hand over the items. "I was just thinking something needs to be done with all of this."

Her mother waited a beat. "How are you this morning?"

"The same as I was yesterday and the day before. Nothing has changed that would make a difference."

"I know, baby." She rubbed her daughter's arm. "It's hard. Come on and get some breakfast."

"I don't want anything to eat." Faith left the bathroom, crawled back into bed, and pulled the covers over her head.

"What time are we going to see my grandchildren today?"

Her shoulders rose and fell with her breath. "I don't feel like going. I'm so exhausted. I'd better get some rest now because when they come home, I won't be able to sleep."

Her mother pulled the comforter back. "I'm not going to let you do this."

"Do what?"

"You cannot disappear from life." She sat on the edge of the bed. "I know you have a lot on you right now, but you can't hide from your reality. You still have to live and you have children to care for, too. They deserve the best you can give them."

Faith grimaced as she sat up in bed, swinging her feet back to the floor. "I know I have to face what's happened. But, I just don't feel like I can right now. This is too much and I feel like I'm losing my mind." As she rested her elbows on her knees, she dropped her head into her hands.

Vonda rubbed her hand across her daughter's back. "Okay. I won't push you. But, you won't be able to function if you don't eat something. How about I fix you some toast and a cup of tea?"

Faith sighed as she lifted her head toward her mother. "If you insist."

"I'll get that ready for you," Vonda said as she patted her daughter on the hand. "You'll get through this. God is right there to help." She left the room, leaving Faith with her thoughts.

Faith considered her mother's comment about God. Her mother always made comments like that. Her belief in God was unwavering. Always had been. Vonda Richards could find God in any situation and seamlessly insert God into any conversation. Faith was raised in church, so she was not without belief in God. However, she wondered how much help He really offered, considering what she was going through.

Faith surveyed the spacious master bedroom. The high tray ceilings, custom wood flooring and sitting area reminded her of the time she and Jamison spent designing their dream home. She looked at the massive, four-poster solid wood bed and matching pieces. All of it was customized per Jamison's specifications. At that moment, Faith realized she couldn't stay in this bedroom. Sleep in this bed. At least, not for the near future. There were way too many memories. She and Jamison had dreamt about their future, spent lazy Saturdays watching movies, and had long conversations in this room. They had made passionate love and conceived their children in this bed. She realized she would have to move to another room. The memories surrounding this room caused a new wave of grief to wash over Faith's soul, causing her to slump to the floor and sob.

"How could this happen? Why did you leave me?" Faith continued to sob. Vonda appeared and sat on the floor beside her daughter. She gathered her in her arms and held her until the crying stopped.

"It just hurts so bad. I don't know if I can make it past this."

"Honey, it may not seem like it right now, but you're going to get through this."

The two sat there for a while longer, rocking back and forth.

Vonda broke the silence, "Let's get off this floor. You just had a C-section, so you probably shouldn't be down here anyway."

Vonda helped her daughter from the floor and onto the side of the bed. "Are you okay?"

"Yes," Faith squeaked out.

"I need to go check your toast. Come on down when you're ready."

Faith remained sitting on the bed for a little while longer. She took some tissue from the box on the nightstand, wiped her face, and blew her nose. Then, she stood and tied her robe around her waist before heading to the kitchen to eat the breakfast her mother prepared for her.

Chapter 23

Faith pulled on her sweatshirt and sweatpants for dinner. She looked down at the items and noticed they were wrinkled. Since she wasn't leaving the house and didn't feel like changing, she felt it was okay. She'd be taking them off and putting her pajamas back on as soon as dinner was over anyway. Her parents and Macie were leaving. Her parents back to California and Macie to Atlanta to start her new job. She thought about putting on some makeup, but didn't have the energy. She opted instead for a tinted lip balm to give her face a little color and allowed her curly hair to hang free. She slipped her feet in her slippers and headed to the dining room.

"I'm really concerned about her," Faith heard Macie say as she approached.

"I haven't seen much of her since the funeral. Getting things in order at The Lewis Agency has taken up a lot of my time. I should've come by and checked on her," Kardel responded.

"All she wants to do is sleep. She hasn't even been to see the children. Bill and I have been going without her. I'm worried she might be depressed," Vonda said.

"I'm thinking about postponing my move to Atlanta again. She needs somebody here, especially when the kids come home."

Vonda looked up from arranging serving dishes on the table. "I agree. Macie, you go on to Atlanta. Bill and I talked last night and decided I'm staying."

"Though I would love to have you all around, I don't want anyone to put their life on hold for me. No one needs to stay." The group turned to see Faith standing in the room. "I'm fine." The glances between her family and friends did not go unnoticed. "Really, I'm okay. Come on. Let's eat."

After the meal was finished and the kitchen cleaned, everyone left, except for Faith's parents.

Faith picked up a stack of mail on the kitchen island. "I guess I need to get through the rest of these cards, so I can get thank you notes out." She took a pink envelope off the top of the stack and opened it. She unfolded the note she found inside and began to read.

You don't know me, but I know you. We have something precious in common: loving and being loved by Jamison. Jamison probably never told you about the son he and I have together, which is the purpose for this note. I know he left a sizable estate behind and I believe my child deserves his fair share. You may think I'm driven by greed, but please know I just want what's right for my and Jamison's child. I'll be in touch.

Faith dropped the note on the counter. "Oh, my goodness." Her hand flew to her mouth.

Vonda came to her daughter's side. "What is it?" She picked up the pink stationery and read the note. "Oh, honey. I'm so sorry."

"I don't need this right now with everything else I have to deal with." She fell into her mother's open arms.

Faith attempted to push back the deluge of tears. She felt the love and support of her family, but also the weight of being a widow and single mother. She felt herself sinking even further emotionally. If she didn't already feel overwhelmed, she did now.

Chapter 24

"I'm so sorry! I didn't know!" Faith yelled. "Nooo! Please! I'm sorry!"

Vonda entered the room and shook her screaming daughter.

"Faith. Faith. Wake up. What's going on?"

"Oh, God. I wish I'd known!" Faith sobbed.

Vonda shook her daughter harder. "You always were hard to wake up. It's okay, honey. Wake up."

Faith blinked her eyes. Finally, she opened them and sat up on the side of the bed. Vonda wrapped her daughter in her arms and waited for her to become fully present. Faith placed her face in her hands and sobbed even harder.

"Oh, Faith," she said, kissing her on the head. "Did you have a nightmare?"

Faith continued crying. She finally reached for some tissue, blew her nose and gathered herself.

Vonda smoothed Faith's hair away from her face. "Are you okay?"

Faith nodded as her heart rate returned to normal. "I had a bad dream. Did I wake you?"

"When I heard you yelling, I came right over to see about you."

"I'm sorry, Mother. You can go on back to bed. I'm okay now."

"Are you sure? You were pretty upset." Vonda went to the other side of the bed. "I think I'll just get in bed with you." She climbed in and Faith laid down and cuddled up next to her.

"Do you want to talk about the dream? It might help."

"I was talking to Jamison."

"About what?"

"He was upset because I wasted time with Evan that I could've spent with him. If I had known our time would be cut short, I never would've taken him for granted the way I did. I wasted months with Evan and I'll never be able to get the time back to spend with Jamison," Faith whimpered.

"Oh, honey. I'm so sorry." Vonda stroked her daughter's hair. "But listen, you have to let that go."

"I feel so guilty. I had a man who loved me and what did I do? I allowed myself to get involved with someone else's husband. I was so wrong and now I'll never be able to fix it."

"Listen to me. You experienced something that is rare. Jamison loved you unconditionally. Even when you thought you were in love with Evan, Jamison still loved you enough to wait for you. Take some solace in the fact he never stopped loving you. He never walked away. You had a lot of beautiful moments with him. Not many people can say that."

"I guess you're right. He looked so angry and hurt in the dream, though. It made me feel bad."

"He's probably angry because you're beating yourself up over something he forgave you for. You can't let this eat you up inside. You need to focus on the happy times. That should keep your mind occupied for a long time."

"I miss him so much. I just can't believe he's gone."

"I know, baby. You're always going to miss him. It'll get easier. Trust me. It will."

"How am I going to make it alone with three children? Huh? How am I supposed to go on without him? We had so many plans and now we won't be able to do any of it. If I'd married him when he first asked me, we might've been able to experience more of those things." Faith broke out with fresh tears.

"Look here, honey. Stop blaming yourself for being human. You made a mistake. That's probably what that dream was about. Jamison's not mad at you, you're mad at yourself. Forgive yourself so you can move on."

Chapter 25

Vonda and Faith valet-parked the car and walked into the hospital entrance. The NICU staff requested a meeting regarding the status of the triplets. They'd been there for four weeks and seemed to be doing well. The fact the staff requested the meeting caused Faith a great deal of concern.

As the women got off the elevator, Vonda took her daughter's hand as they walked down the hallway. "I know you're a little nervous."

"I am, Mother. I just can't take any more bad news. I can barely get out of the bed as it is. I haven't been to see the kids as often as I'd like. If I have one more thing to deal with, I think I might just lock myself in my bedroom and never come out."

"You do understand you can't do that, right?" Vonda squeezed her daughter's hand as they arrived at the office.

"Hi, how can I help you?" the receptionist asked as the women approached the counter.

"We're here for a meeting with Roberta Smith."

"She's wrapping up another meeting, but she shouldn't be long." The receptionist came from around the counter and motioned toward a room around the corner. "Please relax in our lounge. There's coffee, tea and some cookies, if you'd like. I'll let her know you're waiting for her."

"Thank you so much." Faith and Vonda entered the room and took in the stone wall with water trickling down it. Overstuffed chairs and couches lined the room and soft lighting emanated from lamps positioned around the space. The moment the lavender scent hit her nostrils, Faith felt herself relax.

"This is lovely," Vonda said, fixing herself a cup of tea. "Comforting."

A woman breezed into the room carrying a tablet. "Hi, ladies. I'm Roberta Smith. Mrs. Lewis?" She extended her hand to Faith.

"Yes and this is my mother, Vonda Richards."

"Nice to meet you two. We'll just talk here. Let me close the door."

Vonda and Faith settled in with hot beverages and cookies. As they waited for Ms. Smith to begin, Faith sensed the woman's mood change to something more serious.

"As you know, this unit provides specialized care for children like yours, who are born early or have some challenges. We care for the whole child. Though our parents can't always interact with their babies like one might expect in a typical birth situation, the expectation is that they will still need to bond with their child so they feel loved and cared for. It is never our intention for our NICU nursing staff to be the people children learn to depend on." Mrs. Smith paused.

"What are you saying?" Faith asked, uncrossing one leg and crossing the other.

"Mrs. Lewis, we know you lost your husband. Sometimes that's a bit much for people to handle." She looked away for a moment as if to find the right words. "Your children will be released very soon. Our concern is that you won't be in a place where you can adequately care for them when that time comes."

"What?" Vonda and Faith said at the same time.

"There is a concern about substance abuse."

Faith sprang from her seat and chuckled. "Me? Substance abuse? Now that's funny. Did you hear that, Mother?"

Vonda stood next to her daughter and put an arm around her. "I don't know what's going on Ms. Smith, but my daughter doesn't drink and she certainly doesn't have a drug problem."

"I'm sure this is difficult for you, Mrs. Richards, but we have to investigate accusations such as these. We've also noted your absence and other interested parties have as well. Requests have been made to do an assessment to determine if you can provide the level of care and nurturing your children will require."

"With all due respect, Ms. Smith, I am doing the best I can considering what's happened in my life. My emotions are raw and my energy level is low. I am in the process of preparing my home to receive three new people. Sometimes I feel like I'm drowning and there's no one to save me. Now, you're telling me I'm not doing enough. What exactly do you expect me to do?"

"Mrs. Lewis," Ms. Smith leaned forward. "I am not without empathy. However, we have to give weight to the question of who is best capable of taking care of your children. Don't you want that for them?"

"Of course, I do, but who better than me? I'm their mother. You're acting as though I'm a drug addict or I've abandoned them, which is not the case. And, who are the interested parties, anyway?"

"The information came to us from an anonymous source."

"What proof do they have, huh?"

"This is ludicrous," Vonda stated.

Faith took a few steps across the room with her hand on her chin. "Would Davore and Hendrix do something like this?"

"Hmm." Vonda nodded. "I was wondering the same thing."

"The question is what they would get out of it. I know they're upset because they believe Evan and I still have something going on, but would they really try to make me lose my children because of it?" Faith stood with her hand on her chin. She paced in silence. Finally, she looked at Ms. Smith and spoke, "Take Davore and Hendrix Lewis off the visitor list. I think that's best."

Vonda rushed to her daughter. Touching her on the shoulder, she asked, "Are you sure? They are their grandparents."

"I'm sure, Mother." Faith patted her mother's hand as it rested on her shoulder. "Just until everything settles out."

"If you're sure about this," Ms. Smith pulled something up on her tablet. "It's done." Ms. Smith stood and extended her hand toward Vonda and Faith. "It's very nice to meet you ladies. Take care." She left the room, leaving Faith and Vonda wondering what could happen next.

Vonda and Faith headed to the NICU to check in on the children. As they approached the entrance to the unit, Vonda stopped suddenly.

"What's wrong?" Faith asked.

"It looks like we won't have to wait too long to see what the devil is up to. Look." She nodded through a glass window.

Faith looked in the direction her mother was nodding and saw her in-laws being escorted from the NICU. Faith took off in their direction, but her mother grabbed her by the arm. "Don't give them any more ammunition. Maybe we can wait in the relaxation lounge until they leave. I don't think we should be in their presence right now."

"I'm getting tired of tiptoeing around them."

"We have to be wise about this. We don't even know if they're responsible. Let's just wait until you cool down."

Hendrix and Davore exited the area and stood face-to-face with Faith and her mother. No one said a word. Quiet stares formed the extent of their communication.

"Why would you deny us time with the children?" Hendrix asked, breaking the silence.

"Maybe for the same reason you tried to deny me time with them," Faith responded.

Davore and Hendrix looked at Faith with blank stares.

"We won't let you keep our grandbabies away from us. We have grandparents' rights," Davore said.

"You don't have any rights unless I say you do," Faith stated.

The silent staring match resumed for a few moments. Finally, Hendrix took Davore by the elbow and led her away. The war had silently begun.

Chapter 26

Janay pulled into the driveway of the home she'd once shared with Evan and their daughters. It had been their dream home before their lives became a nightmare. She put the vehicle in park and waited for her daughters to come to the door. This was the practice since she'd moved out eighteen months or so ago, when she and Evan separated. After her kidnapping and rape, and then returning to find her husband in a relationship with Faith, Janay tried desperately to remain in her marriage. However, she realized it was way too soon and she needed some healing before she could address that part of her life. So, she'd moved in with her mother, Big Momma and her sister, Cherlynn. The Ns shared time with both parents to provide some normalcy and stability as well.

After waiting for longer than the normal period of time, Janay realized this was not a typical day. She pressed the garage door opener and pulled her car into the garage. She was moving back in with Evan today. Her family would be reunited. She knew there were still issues to work out, but at least they were moving in a positive direction.

She sat in the garage a few more minutes with thoughts whizzing through her head. Was she making the right decision?

Was she ready for this? Was Evan ready to meet her expectations? Could she trust him? In the end, there was no way to answer any of those questions without moving back in and trying it out.

The door opened from the house to the garage and Janay's eyes met Evan's.

"You've been sitting out here for a while. Are you coming in?" The two chuckled as Janay exited the vehicle. She popped open the trunk to retrieve some of her and the Ns' belongings. Evan grabbed her before she could gather them and planted a kiss on her lips, causing Janay's breath to catch in her throat. The emotion it evoked revealed that Evan still had a hold on her heart. She stood with her mouth open while Evan placed his hands in his pocket and looked away.

"I've been wanting to do that for a while. I've missed you. I've missed us."

Janay didn't know how to respond, so she decided not to. Besides, she was still recovering from the kiss her husband laid on her.

Evan interrupted the awkwardness of the moment. "Hey, uh, I'll get these," he said, grabbing the bags from the trunk.

Janay walked into the house without a word while Evan trailed her. Once she entered the family room, she noticed a bottle chilling and two wine glasses.

"What's this?" she asked, finding her voice.

"It's a celebration. You know, for your first night back home."

Janay smiled and felt the concerns she felt earlier melt away. Evan loved her and was committed to trying. She resolved to give her personal best effort as well to give their marriage the every chance possible.

Chapter 27

Faith stood in the door of one of the guest bedrooms and watched as her mother packed. She didn't want her to leave but, under the circumstances, she understood. She still needed her mother's support. She was handling estate concerns, officially shutting her childcare business down and preparing for her triplets' homecoming. Her mother's support was invaluable.

"I'm so sorry I have to go, dear," Vonda said, removing a few pairs of jeans from a drawer.

"I understand. You have to go home sometime. You couldn't stay here forever. Take care of Daddy and don't worry about me."

"I wish Bill would listen to me. I told him to hire someone to work on the roof, but no, he just had to do it himself. Falling off the roof was the last thing we needed. So much for saving money now. We still have to pay to get the roof fixed, but we also have to pay Bill's medical expenses. He's so stubborn and cheap, it makes things more difficult than they have to be sometimes." She sighed and shook her head as she continued to pack. "I'll be back as soon as possible. This really isn't a good time for me to be leaving." Shelooked up at her daughter. "If you need me to come back sooner, just let me know and I'll make arrangements for your dad."

"Mother, you and Dad aren't moving here, are you?"

"I've actually thought about it. Bill doesn't want to deal with the Michigan winters, though."

Faith laughed. "I bet you did consider it. I was trying to make the point that you live in California, so I have to figure out how to make this work on my own."

"You have no idea how much help you're going to need. You need to learn to let people help you. If you don't, you'll be just like your father, hurting yourself for no good reason."

"But, with Macie in Atlanta, you and Dad in California, and Kardel so busy with The Lewis Agency, I don't have a choice." Faith tried to keep her emotions in check. She not only needed but wanted her loved ones around. However, she didn't want anyone feeling guilty about going on with their lives.

"I notice you didn't mention your in-laws. It's too bad they've positioned themselves against you. It would be convenient and helpful if they were involved."

"I know."

"Have you had any contact with them?"

"No, not since we saw them at the hospital."

"Do we know anything more about who wrote the note? I've been wondering about that ever since it arrived."

"No, I don't. It's so nerve-racking not knowing if this woman is telling the truth or not. It might just be a money grab, which is what I suspect."

Faith's shoulders slumped as her mind rehearsed all she had to deal with.

Vonda went to her daughter and took her by the shoulders. "I know it seems like you'll never get through all of this, but stand strong. You've got this." She looked at her watch. "I've got to get to the airport so I don't miss my flight. Are you ready?"

"Just let me grab my purse and get my shoes on."

***

Faith watched as Vonda checked her bags curbside and disappeared into the airport. She pulled the car away from the curb and entered Interstate 94 to begin the drive home. For the first time since the dilemma started, Faith truly felt alone. She asked herself for the fiftieth time how she was going to make it through this. It seemed like more than one person should have to go through.

She felt the problem with Jamison's parents would work itself out. They were experiencing the grief of losing their son as well. Faith wondered if that played a part in their actions.

Raising Mercy, Grace, and Jamison Jr. would be challenging. Faith considered hiring some help to take care of the house, so she could focus on the children. One thing she and Jamison agreed on was they would not allow strangers to raise their children. She would just have to work out a system and stick to it. That was the only way.

Her mind went to the woman who claimed to have Jamison's son. Now, that was an issue she didn't know how to get past. There were so many unanswered questions. She knew in her heart this was not something Jamison would keep from her. The man she knew would never knowingly abandon a child he fathered. He was a man of honor. A man of integrity. However, Faith wondered how this woman seemed to know so much about her. She even knew their home address, which was information she and Jamison worked diligently to keep confidential. How would this woman know where they lived if Jamison didn't tell her? Did he have a moment of indiscretion he hadn't revealed to her? Faith's mind whirled with the possibilities. What if what she thought she and Jamison had was really a make-believe family? Faith pushed those thoughts from her mind. There wasn't much she could do about it anyway. She made a decision to stop by the hospital for a visit before going to her house alone for the very first time since this whole thing started.

***

Faith's visit with her little family was over and she was walking to her car in the hospital's parking structure. When she sat in her car, she looked up to notice a bright pink envelope stuck under her windshield wiper. Immediately, she recognized it as the same color as the note she'd gotten from the mystery woman. Faith looked around to see if she noticed anyone who might be the originator of the notes she'd been getting, but she didn't notice anyone. She snatched it from the windshield, reentered her vehicle and ensured her doors were locked as she read the note.

I don't know exactly what Jamison was worth when he died. However, based on my research, The Lewis Agency alone is worth a few hundred thousand dollars. Taking into account investments, savings, life insurance, and that huge house you live in, my son should be set for life.

My son needs his inheritance and we don't have time to go through the legal process. I will accept no less than five hundred thousand dollars as a settlement. If you don't respond to my demands, I'll go to the press and tell them Jamison was a deadbeat dad who didn't support his child and how you are withholding his rightful portion of his father's estate. I know you don't want Jamison's sterling image tarnished, so I'm sure you'll cooperate. I will provide you with additional directions soon.

Faith felt the façade crumble. Her emotional dam broke. She'd been convincing, but the energy it took to do so finally took its toll on her. The flood of tears that flowed had been building up for weeks. She welcomed the cleansing that came from the deluge. She needed it. It was unnatural and potentially harmful to hold this level of emotion in, but she was concerned that once she released the pressure, she would never be able to regain control of her emotions again. However, if she was going to recover, it was necessary.

Chapter 28

Faith rose early the next morning. There was no bacon cooking and no one else moving about the house — a reminder that her mother had gone home, and she was alone. She laid in bed, trying to determine her agenda for the day.

She reached for the picture of her and Jamison that sat on the nightstand. It was taken on their wedding day. They were so happy. It was evident. Faith ran her hand across it, as if she could actually touch Jamison's face by doing so.

"I'm trying to stay strong, baby, but this is getting to be too much. Your parents are causing problems and there's this woman who says you fathered her child. I wish you could tell me what's going on. Is this woman telling the truth? Did you hide this from me? I can't take any more surprises. I sure hope there aren't any more coming."

Faith placed the picture back on the nightstand and decided to go to the babies' room to see what needed to be done there.

She stepped into the room. Its lavender walls accented the grayish finish on the cribs. She noted the babies' clothing had been washed, but not put away in their drawers. The beds needed fitted sheets. The window coverings were still in the boxes and she needed to contact the installer. She retrieved her cell phone and took note of what needed to be done to make sure the room was ready. She would return after breakfast.

She went to the kitchen and stood with her hands placed on her sides. She considered fixing breakfast, but decided she wasn't hungry. She continued through the house to her childcare room. It had been weeks since this room had seen any use. Since she assumed she would be busy taking care of her children, it wasn't clear when she would use it again. Perhaps, it would make a great play room for her kids once they got a little older. Again, she took out her cell phone and noted some things she needed to do in this space as well.

Faith returned to her bedroom. She decided to shower and change so she could begin tackling her to-do list.

Once in the nursery, Faith folded all the clothing items neatly and placed them in each child's storage area. Next, she lifted a bag she found in the corner of the room. Wondering what was in it, she pulled out three wrapped items. She unwrapped them to find custom engraved wooden signs, one for each child. She surmised Jamison must have purchased them. She smiled because she knew he thought they were necessary to keep everything in order. Everyone's space had to be identifiable. She situated them on the dressers and they looked wonderful since they almost perfectly matched the finish on the furniture.

She put the fitted sheets on the beds and loaded the attached changing tables with diapers, wipes, lap pads and diaper ointment. Afterward, she vacuumed the floor. She looked around the space, and aside from the blinds, the room appeared ready.

148

Faith didn't know what to do next. It was too early to call her mother and Macie was at work, so she decided to go to the hospital for an early visit. She would have lunch after that if she was hungry by then. With her plan in place, she left the house for the next part of her day.

***

Faith entered the area and scanned her wristband to get into the unit. She spent time with each of her children. She was amazed at how they were maturing. Each of them was displaying a unique and individual personality, though they were still so young.

"They're almost ready to leave us. I know you're excited," a voice spoke behind her.

"I am. I'm also a little scared. This is a huge responsibility. I just hope I'm up to the challenge." Faith turned to find the voice belonged to the nurse she'd spoken to previously.

"Don't be afraid. God is with you."

"My mother always says that, but I feel like He abandoned me just when I needed Him."

"He didn't leave you."

"Well, where is He? I don't see Him. I don't feel Him." Faith's voice rose.

"He's right there going through this with you. We have to believe He's there, even if we don't feel or see Him."

Faith thought about the woman's words. There was something about them that gave her peace.

"I guess I've just been so busy feeling sorry for myself, I forgot God was even available to me." Faith felt the heaviness she had been feeling lift. "You have no idea how much you helped me today. Thank you so much."

"You're welcome. It's all a part of my job. Do you have some time? I'd like to show you a few things you'll need to do when these little ones come home."

"Are you kidding me? I have nothing but time. I'd love to stick around and get some tips on how to take care of them." Faith looked over the nurse's shoulder and caught a brief glimpse of someone disappear into a room on the other side of the unit. She felt she'd encountered her before but couldn't place the face. Faith thought perhaps her lack of sleep had caught up with her, so she returned her attention to the nurse. After about an hour, she left the hospital.

Chapter 29

Faith received the phone call she had been waiting for. The triplets were coming home in two days, giving her time to tie up loose ends and complete any remaining preparations for their arrival. She disproved the accusations lodged against her and was free to bring her children home.

Faith felt a strange sense of excitement and anxiety. Excitement because she would be able to touch and hold and love on her children whenever she wanted. She felt anxiety because she truly didn't know what laid ahead. She was about to live the dream she and Jamison had spoken about on so many occasions. They didn't envision triplets but had entertained the idea of having three children. They also didn't consider he wouldn't be there to help raise them.

She gathered the car seats and the triple stroller to be loaded into her vehicle. She realized she would probably need an extra set of hands to make all of this happen, at least for the first time. Faith knew exactly who to call. Kardel. She listened as the phone rang. She knew he would be honored to stand in for his friend in bringing Jamison Jr., Mercy, and Grace home.

"Hey, Faith." Kardel picked up on the first ring.

"Hey, how are things going?"

"Things are going great. How are you?"

"As you might expect, I'm still adjusting." Faith sniffled during their brief silence. "I miss him so much, you know? I never imagined this would be happening."

"I miss him, too." The two were silent for another moment.

Faith gathered herself. "Well, I'm calling because I need your help."

"Anything. You just name it."

"The babies are coming home the day after tomorrow and I need some help."

"I can do anything but that."

"Why? Are you afraid of babies?"

"No. I'm in New York and I won't be back until next week. I sure wish I could be there."

"I wish you could, too."

Faith and Kardel spoke for a while longer, then disconnected their call. Kardel promised to come by for an extended visit when he returned.

Faith had to face the fact that this would be her first adventure as a single parent. She decided to install the car seats' bases and put the triple stroller, along with the carriers in the SUV, so at least that much would be done. She was a little nervous. It all seemed so overwhelming.

Chapter 30

"Daddy, how is Miss Faith doing?"

"I don't know honey. I think she had her babies."

"Babies?"

"Yes, she had three babies at one time."

"Can we call her?"

Evan and Janay glanced at each other. "I don't think so, Honey Bear. She's probably very busy."

Nahla continued eating, seeming to drop the subject.

"She needs our help, Daddy. I can feel it."

"I don't know about that."

"I do. We need to call her."

***

Faith was relaxing and catching up on some of her favorite TV shows when her phone rang. It was Evan's number. She had been forwarding phone calls to voice mail since she hadn't felt much like talking, but today she was in desperate need of some conversation, so she decided to answer.

"Hello."

"Hi, Faith." After an awkward silence, Evan spoke. "I was calling to check on you."

"It's nice of you to reach out to me, but I don't need any more trouble and I know Janay would not want you talking to me. So, I think we need to end this call right now."

Evan chuckled. "I understand, but it's okay. Really. As a matter of fact, I have you on speaker. Janay can hear everything we say."

Unconvinced, Faith responded, "Right."

"Janay, will you please tell her?"

"Evan is telling the truth. Now listen, I'm not crazy about you still being in our lives, but I'm tired of trying to keep you out. Evan is concerned about you and Nahla is behind this phone call."

"Wow. I don't know what to say."

"Janay and I are rebuilding our marriage," Evan explained.

"I'm learning to trust him. That's the only way we're going to make this work. So, here we are. By the way, I'm sorry to hear about Jamison. He seemed like a wonderful man. Congratulations on the triplets."

"Thank you. They'll be coming home tomorrow."

"Is there anything I can do to help?" Evan asked.

"No, is there anything *we* can do to help. I've made progress, but I'm not perfect," Janay corrected her husband.

"I appreciate your offer but I think I can handle it."

"What do you have going on tomorrow, Janay?"

"Naomi's still not feeling well, so I'll be home with her. Why?"

"I was thinking we could help Faith."

"Aren't you working tomorrow?"

"Yes, but I can take some time off. I don't want Faith to manage this alone."

There were a few silent moments. Then Janay spoke. "I'll see if Big Momma will watch Naomi. If not, you can go. But, please don't make me regret it."

"You don't have to go alone, Faith. Just tell me what time to meet you and one or both of us will be there."

***

The next day Faith drove to the hospital, excited about beginning her new journey. She'd changed her mind a few times about allowing Evan to escort her. Each time she called to tell him she didn't want to impose on him, he was patient with her, reassured her it wasn't an imposition, and told her he would still be there. In the end, she decided to accept the support.

She was surprised by Janay's change of heart. Not even a year ago, she was sneering at her in the drug store. Now, she seemed willing to help and even allowed Evan to help her. Apparently, she was getting better and that was good news.

Faith was happy Janay and Evan were working on their relationship. It bothered her that she was partially responsible for the problems in the Ingram marriage. She would never put herself in that position again. Marriage was sacred. Something she knew all too well now.

She pulled into the valet parking lane in front of the hospital and removed the stroller and car seats. She attached the car seats to the stroller and entered the hospital. Upon entering, she saw Evan in the vast lobby. He looked up as she approached him.

"Hey, pretty lady."

Evan opened his arms and drew Faith in. "Hi, Evan." Faith rested there for a few moments, enjoying the closeness.

"Today's the big day, huh?"

"Yes, it is."

"Where do we need to go?" Evan examined the stroller. "Whoa, that is one big stroller." The pair shared a laugh.

"See, Hendrix? It's a good thing the nurses were still able to keep us up-to-date about the babies. Otherwise, we wouldn't have known they were being released today." Faith followed the sound of the voice and found her mother-in-law's teary eyes. "I knew there was something going on. He's here, but she didn't even ask us to come. How could you do this?" Faith's mouth dropped open. She walked toward her in-laws as Hendrix tried to pull Davore away. Evan reached for Faith as she whipped around him.

Faith spoke to her in-laws through clenched teeth. "I have done everything I know to do to be respectful. I have taken your insults. I have ignored your ridiculous accusations. But, I have had enough. I loved Jamison as hard and as heavy as I could and he loved me the same way. I was faithful to him." She placed her hands on her hips. "You know, I'm trying to figure out why you care enough to come here to visit an expression of a love you don't accept. Now, listen here. You will either show me some respect or prepare to never see Jamison Jr., Grace, and Mercy again. Please don't make me prove that I'll do that."

"Is that a threat?" Davore asked.

"I'm going to have peace and if your presence interferes with that, well, you can figure out the rest."

"I suppose Evan gives you peace, huh?" Davore asked.

"You two are so concerned about Evan. He's a friend who volunteered to help, unlike the two of you. You're just make-believe family, because true family wouldn't treat me the way you do."

Hendrix stepped forward. "Faith, I think you'd better—"

"And another thing. You have some nerve telling the people at this hospital that I was a drunk and that I wasn't spending enough time with my kids, when you have done nothing to help me one bit. You ought to be ashamed."

"Wait a minute." Hendrix's voice rose as he moved between his wife and daughter-in-law. "I don't know what you're talking about."

"Maybe you should ask your wife," Faith said, jabbing her finger toward her mother-in-law.

157

"I don't know what you're talking about, either," Davore said.

"I don't know what kind of game you're playing, but you will not harass me anymore. That's over." Faith turned to continue toward the elevator, leaving Davore and Hendrix flabbergasted.

Faith led the way as she and Evan took the elevator to the fifth floor. Once there, Faith went to the nurse's station to get the release process started.

"Good morning," she said, smiling.

The nurse sitting behind the counter looked up. "Good morning, Mrs. Lewis. I bet you're here to take those adorable babies home today." She whipped around in her chair and looked toward a group of cubicles behind her. "Let's go right over here."

"I'll wait out here," Evan said, pointing at a bank of chairs.

"No, you don't have to do that. Come on."

As Faith followed the woman, she noticed someone abruptly turn and head in a different direction. "Excuse me." She headed toward the woman who stopped, but didn't face her. Faith positioned herself in front of her. "Do I know you from somewhere? You look so familiar."

The woman displayed a nervous smile. "No, I don't think we've met. I must have a twin out there somewhere."

"I'm sure I've seen you somewhere before..." Faith searched for the nametag on the woman's smock before continuing. "Tisa. Maybe I've just seen you around here. It was nice meeting you."

Faith went to the office and Evan followed with the triple stroller in tow. He parked it outside the office and stepped inside, where he sat beside Faith. After everything was completed, Faith and Evan moved to the area where the babies were. After Faith prepared each child to leave, she carefully placed them in the stroller and Evan fastened them in.

Faith drove home, looking in the rear-view mirror every time one of the infants made a noise. She slowed her vehicle way ahead of every stop light. Her stomach flipped when one of the babies began crying. *What was she supposed to do? Was she supposed to pull over to check on the child?* She decided to pull over in a nearby parking lot to ensure everything was okay.

Evan pulled up behind her and leaped from his vehicle. He ran to Faith's side. "Is everything okay?"

Faith sighed. "I heard crying and decided to check it out."

Evan chuckled. "You can't do that every time one of them starts crying. If you do, you'll never get where you're trying to go. Trust me. They will live."

"Don't laugh at me." Faith joined in the laughter.

"Get back in," he said, shaking his head as he headed back to his vehicle. "All is well."

Faith pulled her SUV into the long driveway leading to her home. When she looked in her rear-view mirror to see if Evan was still behind her, she saw his jaws drop as he took in the home she and Jamison built. She went into the garage and he parked in the driveway.

"Wow! I didn't know how lucrative being a private investigator was. This is a beautiful home."

"Thank you. It seems a little overwhelming and lonely without him. Living here with all those memories is difficult. But, it's paid off thanks to the policy Jamison purchased, so I'll be staying here for a while."

Evan's phone rang. "Hey Janay, we're just getting to Faith's house. I'm going to help her get them settled, then I'll be home." Faith listened as he spoke with his wife. She found herself feeling a little jealous that they had each other to talk to. "That's not a problem. If you order the pizza in about fifteen or twenty minutes, I'll pick it up. Love you, too."

Evan disconnected the call and looked at Faith. "Are you okay?" he asked. "You're crying."

It was then Faith realized there were indeed tears rolling down her face. She wiped them with the back of her hand as Evan approached her. "I really miss having those kinds of conversations with Jamison. You have no idea how blessed you are to have Janay in your life."

"You can have that again, Faith. You're a wonderful, caring, attractive woman. Any man would be very happy to have you as a wife. I should know."

Faith looked away then turned her attention back to her SUV. She still hadn't wrapped her mind around being a widow, let alone remarriage. After all, she now had three other lives to care for and she was sure they would occupy the bulk of her time and energy.

"Well, I guess we'd better get these little people in the house, so you can get back to your family."

Evan took two of the carriers, leaving Faith to carry one. They went upstairs into the children's suite and placed them in their cribs. Then, Faith led Evan back downstairs to the front entrance.

"By the way, I heard what Jamison's parents said. In order to inflict that type of pain on you, they have to be feeling at least that level of pain themselves. People can only give you what they have on the inside of them. Don't take it to heart."

"I hear what you're saying, but it doesn't excuse them. I won't let them disturb what little peace I have. It's all I have left now." An awkward silence ensued. "I really appreciate your help today. Please tell Janay I said thank you for loaning you to me. It turns out I really needed the help."

"No problem. Don't hesitate to call if you need anything else."

Crying rang out from the nursery.

"Thanks, but I think I can take it from here." Evan smiled at her as he exited the home. Faith fell against the door, closing it. As she jogged up the stairs, she said, "I guess it's time to get this party started."

Chapter 31

Faith stood at her kitchen counter preparing bottles for her children. While all three babies were asleep, a rarity, she decided to prepare herself a cup of coffee and a small meal. Since it was forecasted to be a nice day out, she planned to take the children for a stroll around the neighborhood. She was experiencing a little cabin fever and needed the fresh air herself. She also believed it would give her a chance to clear her mind a little.

It had been almost a month since she brought Mercy, Grace and Jamison Jr. home from the hospital. Though she had been extremely nervous about being able to care for them on her own, everything was working out better than she expected. No one had gotten sick, no one had swallowed anything they weren't supposed to, and she hadn't lost her mind.

The family was finally settling into a routine, which was helpful for Faith. She was able to do what needed to be done without the exhaustion. If all three cooperated with a naptime schedule, it would make things even easier. However, it always seemed like one of them refused to participate. Faith would continue working with them since it was important for everyone.

Her doorbell rang and she wondered who it could be, since she didn't expect anyone. She viewed the individual via the security camera but didn't recognize him. She decided to use the intercom to find out who he was and what he wanted, instead of opening her door.

"Hi, can I help you?"

The man looked around as if looking for the source of the voice. Finally, he spotted the camera and responded, "Hi, are you Faith Lewis?" he asked with a smile. His teeth were so white they sparkled, even on camera.

"Who's asking?"

"I have some paperwork I need to give her. That's all." Again, his smile blinded her.

"What kind of paperwork?"

"They don't tell us all of that."

"So, you're a process server?"

"Maybe. Are you Faith Lewis?"

"Yes. Hold on a second and I'll open the door."

Faith grabbed her cell phone and placed a call. Kardel answered right away.

"Hey, Faith."

"Hey. Listen, there's someone at my door who I believe is a process server. I just wanted to have someone on the line when I open the door, in case something goes bad."

"Did he threaten you?"

"No, actually he's pretty friendly. I'm just a little suspicious, with so much going on."

"Go ahead and open the door. It's probably okay."

Faith opened the door. "Ma'am, are you Faith Lewis?"

"Yes, I am."

He handed her some paperwork. "You've been served. Have a great day." The man hopped back into his car. Faith assumed he was headed to serve the next victim.

"Did you hear?" Faith asked Kardel.

"Yeah, I heard. Who's it from?"

She felt her heart race as she reviewed the paperwork. Her mouth dropped as she read the contents. Faith couldn't believe what she was reading.

"It's my in-laws. It seems they initiated a proceeding asserting their rights as grandparents. I can't believe this."

"Wow, that's pretty cold."

"Well, it's just one more thing I have to deal with. I'll let you go so you can get back to what you were doing."

"No problem. Hang in there. Everything's going to be all right."

"I hope so. Thank you for your support. It means the world to me."

"It's never a problem. I'll talk to you soon."

Faith returned to the kitchen and prepared her coffee. She settled herself at the kitchen table and picked up her cell phone to place another call. "Hello," Vonda said.

"Hey, Mother. What are you doing?"

"I'm just relaxing a little. How are my grandchildren doing?"

"They're fine. They're all asleep for once."

"I sure wish I was there. I'm missing them grow up."

"You can come anytime you want. It'll be awhile before I try to manage getting all four of us on a plane to come out there."

Vonda and her daughter laughed. "I understand."

"I just called to let you know the latest."

"What happened?"

"Hendrix and Davore filed a case to assert their grandparents' rights. Can you believe that? I was served a few minutes ago."

"Why did they have to take the legal route, when they could have just called you and tried to work things out?"

Faith was silent for a few moments, counting the attempts the Lewises had made to see the children. "They've called and left messages, asking to see them, but I haven't returned their calls. I just don't want to deal with them."

Vonda sighed. "I know they haven't behaved the best, but do you think keeping the babies from them is the best way for you to respond?" Again, Faith was quiet as she thought about what her mother said. "Look at it from their perspective. They lost their son. Those babies are the only connection they have left to Jamison. They don't want to lose them, too."

"But, I'm their mother and Jamison's widow. They don't even like me. Why should I let them into my space?"

"I agree they need to at least be cordial and certainly you are due their respect. It sounds like you might have to deal with them anyway. You've forced their hand. Now, it'll be up to a judge to decide, unless the three of you can work it out before you go to court. I highly recommend you contact them and at least try to come up with some type of agreement where they can see their grandchildren."

"I'll think about it. I knew I should've called Macie. She would've taken my side." Mother and daughter chuckled.

"You called the right person. I'll talk to you later. Bill is calling for me and I need to see what he wants."

"Okay, Mother. I'll talk to you again soon."

Faith disconnected the call. Her mother had given her food for thought. She went to the babies' suite and watched as they slept. It was a joy watching them interact with their world. She couldn't imagine missing any of this. She would spend time considering her mother's point as she promised. If she decided to let the senior Lewises back in, it would be on a probationary basis, considering their behavior before and since Jamison passed away. She decided to contact her lawyer to let him know about this new wrinkle as well, just in case things ended up in court.

Chapter 32

"What's going on, girl? How are my little stars?" Macie asked.

"They're great. They're tiring me out but that's to be expected," Faith responded. The truth was, she was exhausted. She hadn't managed to completely get them all on the same schedule yet. She was attending to one baby or another almost twenty-four hours a day. "How's the new job going?"

"It's good."

Faith waited for Macie to elaborate. When that didn't happen, she said, "You don't sound too excited about it. What's wrong?"

"I really miss home. I thought I would enjoy the Georgia weather and the change of scenery, but it turns out it's not what I was expecting."

"Um-hmm. I think you're missing a certain man who's running The Lewis Agency, too."

"Maybe."

"That's what I thought."

"I like Kardel and I would love to get to know him better."

"But—" Faith interjected.

"But we barely talk and there's been no mention of a visit."

"I know he's been extra busy with The Lewis Agency since Jamison passed. He didn't even have time to go with me to bring the babies home and you know that's not like him. Don't give up on him. I'm sure he'll have more time soon."

"We'll see. Hey, have you gotten any more notes?"

"Yes and it's freaking me out. The last one was taped to my front door. Another one was on my windshield at the hospital. How does this woman know where to find me?"

"Who said it was a woman?"

"Jamison was not gay. You can trust me on that. Plus, the note said we'd both been loved by Jamison and we both have a child by him."

"Anyone can write anything on a note. It could be a man trying to get some money from you."

"I hadn't thought of that."

"That's what you have me for. What are the notes saying?"

"She's threatening to expose Jamison as a deadbeat dad if I don't give her a half-million dollars. Oh, and she's also going to tell people that I'm a greedy widow, who is refusing to give her son his fair share of his father's estate."

"What? You need to call the police. That's blackmail."

"If she keeps on pressing me, I will. I just have so much going on, I can barely think straight. I haven't even told you about the Lewises."

"What are Davore and Hendrix up to now?"

"They're demanding grandparents' rights."

"What?"

"Yes, they had me served and everything. Mother says I should just cooperate instead of fighting it, but I haven't decided what I'm going to do yet."

"Girl, this is too much. Keep me in the loop. I might need to come up there and whoop somebody."

"I will, but you can keep the whooping. I don't need any more problems. I love you, girl."

"I love you back."

Faith thought about the notes and the woman who sent them, and an idea came to mind. Something she wished she'd thought of earlier and was surprised she hadn't. She knew just who to call to find out the truth. She pressed the name on her cell phone and waited for an answer.

"Hey, Faith. How are you doing?" Kardel answered.

"Hey. I'm doing well."

"I'm calling because I need to talk to you about these notes I've been getting."

"Hold on. What notes?"

"I've been getting letters from someone saying they felt they were entitled to a share of Jamison's estate and had a son by him."

"What? How long has this been going on?"

"It started shortly after Jamison passed away."

"You should've told me about that when it first started."

"You're right. I should've. But, there was so much going on it didn't even cross my mind. I didn't take it seriously until she demanded a half-million dollars, or she would put all of this bad information out about Jamison being a deadbeat dad and me being a spiteful stepmother, who was keeping her son from getting his fair share."

"Wow."

"Since you're Jamison's closest friend, can you think of who this might be? Someone who was in a serious relationship with him?"

"Jamison wasn't a man who had a lot of relationships with women." Kardel was quiet for a moment. "But, there was one woman. Tisa Alexander. He fell in love with her and even asked her to marry him. She said no. Jamison suspected it was because she met someone who had more money than he did at the time. They broke up, then that's when Jamison met you."

"This woman says she has a son by him. Is that true?"

"She didn't have one when they broke up and Jamison never mentioned one to me."

"Tisa. Why does that name sound familiar?"

"Maybe Jamison mentioned her."

"No, I don't think so. I'm trying to understand her motive."

"If it's Tisa, she is an opportunist, plain and simple. Jamison was willing to give her the world. Now he's gone and she sees another opportunity. Whatever you do, don't give Tisa a dime. I'll look into it and see if I can find out anything on her."

"I just don't understand why all of this is happening."

"We'll get it figured out. Make sure you let me know if anything else comes up."

"I will. Thanks for answering my questions."

"All right. Someone came into the office, so I have to go. I'll talk to you soon."

"I'll talk to you later."

Faith and Kardel disconnected their phone call. Faith's mind was whirling even more. She didn't know what to think. She was committed to getting to the bottom of it, so she could get on with her life.

Chapter 33

Faith rushed to the door with two children in her arms, one on each shoulder. She used the camera located high up over the door, to determine who was banging on the door and ringing the doorbell incessantly. When she realized who it was, she considered whether she wanted to let them in. It wasn't her first choice, but she realized she could only hold them off for so long. It wasn't the best time for them to visit, considering her hair was all over her head, she had yet to shower or brush her teeth and she just didn't feel like dealing with their pompous attitudes.

The strain from dealing with the unknown woman making demands, caring for three babies and grieving Jamison's death had all taken their toll on her. Now, the other source of stress was at her door demanding to visit their grandchildren.

"Faith, please open the door," she heard Hendrix say.

"In case you forgot, you filed a lawsuit against me. Unless a judge says I have to let you visit, I don't think you should be here. In fact, you should be talking to my lawyer."

"Please. We've already dropped that lawsuit. We want to do what we should've done in the first place. Talk. We're family, whether we want to be or not."

Faith thought about what Hendrix was saying in the context of her mother's advice. Maybe it would be best if she heard them out and they heard her out as well. She released the breath she didn't realize she was holding. She decided to do just what he asked and determine if things would go further. She managed to unlock and open the door, revealing Hendrix and Davore with their heads hung low.

"Hello," Faith coldly said.

"Hi," the senior Lewises said in unison. An awkward silence hung in the air. "Can we come in?" Hendrix asked.

"Look, I don't want to fight with you," Faith began. "So, if that's what you're here for, we need to say goodbye."

"Please. We're not here to fight," Davore said. Faith noticed her eyes were glued to the babies on her shoulder.

"We just want to see our grandbabies and talk to you for a bit. We promise we won't stay long," Hendrix pleaded.

Faith stepped aside, allowing her in-laws entry into her home. After she pressed her back against the door to close it, she led them into the family room where the third baby was cooing in a bassinette.

Davore stood over Jamison Jr and the child smiled at her. "May I?" she asked, glancing at Faith.

"Sure."

Davore picked up the boy and cradled him close. She inhaled and smiled as she stroked the back of his head.

Faith faced her father-in-law. "Would you like to hold her?" she asked, offering Grace to him.

"I sure would."

Faith released Grace to her grandfather. She began to cry, unappreciative of being disturbed. Faith watched as Jamison's parents played with their grandchildren. They seemed amazed by them.

Faith broke the silence. "They're precious, aren't they?"

Davore's voice broke as she responded, "They remind me of Jamison. I miss my son so much. It's hard to believe he's gone."

Faith watched as Hendrix attempted to soothe his wife, though his own pain was evident.

"This is probably the most difficult thing I've ever had to deal with and I've encountered a lot in my lifetime. The possibility of losing my son never even crossed my mind," Hendrix said.

Davore looked over at Faith. "I can't imagine things have been easy for you either."

"Things have been extremely difficult. Some days the weight of what's happened causes me to want to stay in bed, but I can't because of them." She gestured toward the babies.

Davore and Hendrix shared a moment where they looked at each other. Hendrix finally spoke, "We wanted to come here to discuss what's going on between us. Things got out of control and we want to see if we can fix it."

Faith leaned back in her seat and folded her arms before asking, "Why did you file that lawsuit against me in the first place?"

"Because we felt you were trying to shut us out," Davore responded.

Faith scooted to the edge of her seat. "Shutting you out? You almost got me shut out of my own children's lives because of your lies. How did you think I would react?"

"You keep saying that, but we don't know what you're talking about," Hendrix insisted.

"Who else would do that?" Faith yelled.

"We don't know, but we didn't." Davore raised her voice.

The adults in the room quieted themselves as Mercy and Grace cried out.

Faith weighed their response and wondered if perhaps they were telling the truth. She acknowledged their consistent response to this issue, but who else would do something like that?

"A lot has happened and it's got us all emotional and probably a little stressed out. Let's calm down so we can think clearly," Davore said, rocking Jamison Jr.

"Before we go any further, I need you two to understand one thing. The only way we're going to be able to go forward is for us to clear the air about how you two seem to feel about me, personally. You don't like me. You've disrespected me. In fact, I don't think you wanted Jamison to marry me."

"We were very concerned about your intentions where our son was concerned. Jamison had been through a lot in his previous relationships, so when you came along we were very cautious. Jamison wasn't, though. His heart was so trusting, he just couldn't imagine he would get hurt or taken advantage of." Davore smiled. "When you developed that relationship with Evan, it troubled us. Then all of this happened: the marriage, this house and these babies. We thought you were taking advantage of him."

"I loved Jamison and would never hurt him that way," Faith explained, then tilting her head to the side continued, "But, don't you think he was a little old for you to be protecting him?"

Davore chuckled. "You would think, but it's not so. You see, it wasn't personal. We were just being a little overprotective. That's all."

Faith thought about Davore's explanation. Something about it seemed inauthentic. Like she was leaving out some details.

Faith rose to put Mercy in the bassinette previously occupied by Jamison, who was sleeping in his grandmother's arms. "I want to show you something." Faith retrieved the pink letters she'd been receiving. She held them up for them to see. "I've been getting these letters from a woman who claims she has a son by Jamison, demanding a huge sum of money from me. I spoke to Kardel and he mentioned they could be from a woman Jamison dated, named Tisa Alexander. Do you know her?"

Faith didn't miss the look Davore shot at Hendrix. It was confirmation something was going on with this Tisa story.

"Um, no. I've never heard of her. If she dated Jamison, their relationship must not have been serious enough for him to introduce her to us," Davore mentioned, focusing her attention on JJ.

"Really? I just thought I'd ask."

Davore returned her attention to Faith. "I hope you can forgive us for how we've acted."

Faith thought for a moment about all Davore and Hendrix had put her through. Though she wanted to protect herself, she knew pain was a part of the human experience. The right thing to do was to forgive and move on. After all, they all needed each other. "Yes, you're forgiven." Faith rose. "I need to get the babies ready for bed." She reached for Jamison Jr.

"Please, let us help you get them ready. We've already missed out on so much."

"Absolutely. Let's get them upstairs."

Faith led her in-laws up to the babies' suite.

Davore and Hendrix marveled at the spacious room their grandchildren resided in. "This is beautiful. I love the way you decorated this room. It's perfect," Davore said, looking around the room.

"Jamison and I picked a lot of this out before he passed away. All I had to do was put it all in place. I think it turned out great."

"You two did a good job," Hendrix stated, surveying the room.

The trio undressed the babies, bathed them and dressed them in their pajamas. They put them to bed and left the suite.

"Well, we'd better go," Hendrix said, reaching out to embrace his daughter-in-law. "We don't want to overstay our welcome.

Faith hugged her father-in-law and spoke, "You all are welcome any time. I'm glad you two came and we were able to work things out. Next time, maybe we can come visit the two of you."

Davore clasped her hands together and said, "That would be so nice. I look forward to it."

"It's a plan then."

Once Davore and Hendrix left the home, Faith turned off the downstairs lights and retired to her bedroom.

***

Faith arose the following morning with a renewed vigor. She'd been thinking about the visit with her in-laws the night before. She felt a sense of peace and joy regarding their reconciliation. She needed them and truthfully, they needed her, too. She hoped they could remain in a good place because her children needed all of the family and friends possible. Not just because of the physical support they could provide in handling three children, but because of the love they could give the children.

Faith already knew Jamison Jr. would have different needs than Mercy and Grace. She knew Kardel would be involved, but one day he would have his own family and they would take precedence. Thankfully, her father was still alive, but he lived in California. It was a good thing Hendrix was local and would be readily available.

She'd laid awake for a while after the Lewises left. They said they had never heard of Tisa Alexander. How could they not know anything about the woman Kardel said their son had a serious relationship with? Something about their story wouldn't let her rest. Just when she shut her eyes, she connected the dots and figured out who Tisa was. She decided she would confront her as soon as she could to end the harassment and get on with her life.

Faith called Davore and Hendrix to ask if they would be willing to babysit while she went to confirm her belief. After she showered, she pulled on a lounger and went to prepare the babies for the day. She walked into the room and as usual, Jamison Jr. was awake, smiling, talking, and sucking his fingers. He was the happiest of the three and loved to be cuddled and talked to. He was focused on something next to his crib and didn't notice her. This happened often and Faith wondered what held his attention. She decided to start with him first since he was already awake.

She moved on to Mercy, who Faith knew would resist waking up but would quickly acquiesce. Grace would be last because she fought being disturbed fiercely. She turned on the mobiles for each child while she went to prepare breakfast for the family.

When her in-laws arrived, she answered the door having done her hair, dressed in a pantsuit, and pulled on heels. Faith felt like her "pre-child" self since she rarely, if ever, dressed like this since giving birth.

She directed the car toward her destination and looked forward to dealing with this issue once and for all. Hopefully, after this, she could close the door on this portion of her life and move on.

She pulled in to the valet parking lane and entered the building. The clicking of her heels echoed through the entry area. When she got off the elevator on the fifth floor, she looked around and realized she hadn't thought this part through. But, not to be discouraged, she decided to start with Ms. Smith's office. If that didn't work, she would figure out the next step. She pushed the button on the intercom by the entrance to the unit. The receptionist allowed her access after she explained her need to see Ms. Smith.

"Hi, Mrs. Lewis," Ms. Smith's receptionist said. "I thought your children were released."

"They were. But, I'm here to see Ms. Smith, if she's available."

"Let me get her for you." The receptionist picked up the phone and seconds later, Ms. Smith appeared.

"Good morning. Come on back. Would you like something to drink?"

"No, I'm okay. Thank you for asking."

Ms. Smith closed the door behind the two and settled in to hear what her visitor had to say.

"How are those beautiful babies of yours?"

"They are wonderful. They're a lot of work, but I'm loving every minute of it. Thank you for all your staff did for them."

"No problem. It's our job." Ms. Smith leaned over her desk. "I must say, I'm surprised to see you. Tell me what I can do for you."

"I know you can't tell me who filed that complaint against me but I think I know. I suspect one of the employees in this department is responsible for that and for leaving harassing notes on my vehicle and at my home."

"That's quite an accusation. Why do you think someone here is doing this?"

"I found out this person had a previous relationship with my husband. Because she works here in this department, she has access to personal information, such as my address. She would also know when I was visiting, so she could put the notes on my car."

"I can see why you would think this person might send you the notes, but why file the complaint?"

"I'm not so sure about that. I'd like to talk to her if I could. Her name is Tisa Alexander."

"We do have a social worker here by that name. But, in situations like this, the hospital has jurisdiction over this situation. I assure you, we'll check into it. If what you're saying is true, it would be considered a breach of our policy and the hospital will take appropriate action."

Faith rose from her seat. "I guess I'll have to trust you'll take care of it. I'd really like to know why she came against me like that. Is it possible you'll be able to share that information with me?"

"I'm not promising anything, but I'll see what I can do."

Faith left the office and headed toward the exit of the unit. Before she reached the door, she saw Tisa. She headed past the door to the other side of the unit. When the woman saw Faith, she increased her pace.

"Tisa! Hi! Can I speak to you for a moment?" Faith asked, keeping her eyes on the woman.

Tisa turned to face Faith. "Oh, hi. Faith, right? W-w-w-what can I do for you?" The woman smiled at Faith, who returned the favor. Faith realized, for the first time, this was the woman who wanted the casket reopened at Jamison's funeral.

"Do you have a few minutes? I'd love to speak with you."

"Um, I guess so. Maybe we can talk in the relaxation room."

"You lead the way," Faith said, gesturing for Tisa to go ahead of her.

The two women went into the space and Tisa fastened the door behind them. Once inside, Faith sat on a couch, reached into her purse and pulled out every note she'd received and laid them out on the table in front of her. Tisa's eyes bugged once they landed on the letters.

Tisa lingered close to the door before meandering toward the seat in front of Faith, who asked, "Do you know why I'm here?"

Tisa lifted her chin and said, "No, I'm sorry I don't."

"I think you do." Faith nodded as she opened one of the notes and read it to the woman. "What do you think about that?"

"I don't think anything about it."

"Do you know my late husband, Jamison Lewis?" Faith looked deep into the woman's eyes.

"I've heard of him. He ran The Lewis Agency, right? My condolences for your loss."

"Thank you. By the way, thank you for coming to pay your respects. I'm sure he would have appreciated it, too."

"Mrs. Lewis, I have things to do today. I can't sit here and talk with you. If there's nothing else…" Tisa scooted to the edge of the chair.

"Please, just humor me for a few more minutes. I had a conversation with my husband's friend and he spoke of a relationship Jamison had some years ago with a woman named Tisa. I think that's quite a coincidence. Don't you?"

"It must be, because I never met your husband."

Faith scooted to the edge of her seat and leaned forward. "Look, let's get to the point. Why are you harassing me? Why did you file that complaint about me not being here for my kids? You almost got them put into foster care, but you knew that could happen because you're a social worker."

Tisa looked away as her facial expression changed. The once stressed face morphed into one of indignation. "I don't owe you an explanation or anything else, but you owe me everything."

"Really. What do I owe you?" Faith said with raised eyebrows.

"It should've been me living the life you did with Jamison."

"What does that have to do with me? I'm not the reason you and Jamison didn't get married. It was your greed that caused it." Tisa's mouth flew open. "Yeah, I know about that."

Tisa recovered quickly. "Oh, really? What else do you think you know?"

"I know Jamison's best friend said he doesn't know anything about you having a child by Jamison. On top of that, my in-laws said they don't even know you."

Tisa threw her head back and let laughter ring out. "Oh, is that what Davore and Hendrix told you?"

If my in-laws don't know her, how does she know their names? "Yes, what's so funny about that?"

"Ask your in-laws."

"I don't have to ask them anything. Jamison would never abandon a child he fathered like you imply he did. You messed up with Jamison, he moved on, married me and now you think I owe you part of my husband's estate. I'd say you are really wrong."

"We'll see about that. My lawyer says—"

"I'm not worried about you or your lawyer, honey."

"You should be. I'm going to get what belongs to Jamison's son."

"Since you obviously need someone to talk some sense into you, I'll help you out. You were never married to Jamison, so you're not entitled to anything. Your child couldn't be Jamison's. He would never abandon a child that was his. You have no standing. No judge in the world will take your claim seriously." She leaned closer to the woman across from her and whispered, "I suggest you leave me alone. You don't want any of this. Trust me."

Faith gathered the letters and put them back in her purse. "I'll just take these in case you don't take my advice. Have a good day," she said, with smugness on her face. Faith strutted out of the room leaving Tisa with a smirk on her face, making Faith nervous.

Faith almost skipped to her vehicle. She felt so much lighter knowing she probably wouldn't have to deal with Miss Tisa again. This season of her life had her in a whirlwind she hoped would soon stop swirling. Between Jamison's death, the babies being premature, this Tisa drama and the issues with her in-laws, her emotions had been all over the place. At times, she thought she would lose her mind.

As she drove, the conversation with Tisa replayed in her mind. It bothered her that the woman seemed so sure of herself. She even implied Davore and Hendrix weren't being truthful with her about Tisa and Jamison's relationship, and maybe even Tisa's son. She wondered if her reunion with the senior Lewises was premature, based on a lie.

Chapter 34

Faith pulled up in her driveway, pressed the button to open the garage door, entered and turned off her vehicle. She exhaled as she thought about the conversation she needed to have with her in-laws. She wasn't excited about it at all, considering she didn't know what she would hear.

She exited the vehicle and entered her home. She found Davore and Hendrix playing with the children in the family room. Everyone looked overjoyed.

"Hi, everyone," she said, flicking JJ's chin. The child laughed at her. He brought her so much joy. "I hope they weren't too much trouble for you."

"Never. We enjoyed being with them. We look forward to spending more time with them," Davore said as she handed Mercy to her mother.

"That would be wonderful."

"It's time for me to put them down for a nap."

"We'll help you."

Once the trio returned to the family room. Hendrix asked, "Did you get your business taken care of?"

Faith motioned for her in-laws to take a seat. "Yes, I did. As a matter of fact, I went to talk to Tisa." Davore and Hendrix shared a quick glance. "She said some things that were different than what you told me."

"We don't know anything about this woman, so whatever she said can't be true," Davore responded.

"I'm having difficulty believing you."

"Are you calling us liars?"

"No, I'm wondering what you're hiding from me and why." After a few moments without a response, Faith continued. "I feel like I'm missing something and quite frankly, I'm getting to the point I don't trust you." She folded her arms and paced the floor. "I'm sorry, but that's how I feel."

The room remained silent.

Davore dropped her head in her hands and spoke, her voice breaking. "We don't know her."

"Davore, she knows your names. How could you not know her? Why won't you just tell me the truth?"

Hendrix cleared his throat. After Davore didn't respond, he said, "Are you going to tell her or am I?" Davore turned away after hearing her husband's comment. "I never should've let things get this far." Again, Davore was silent. "All right, I'll tell her," Hendrix said.

"No, I'll do it." Davore rolled her eyes at Hendrix. "You just couldn't keep your mouth shut." She straightened her back and

187

focused on her daughter-in-law. "To answer your question, yes, we know who Tisa is."

"Finally, the truth."

"Jamison was in love with Tisa. They were always together. They would beam when they were with each other. I'd never seen Jamison happier than when he was with her. After a couple of years, he proposed and Tisa said yes." Davore drew a deep breath and released it. "A few months into the engagement, Jamison told us the wedding was off. He wouldn't explain why, but we could see he was absolutely devastated."

"I never knew about that," Faith said.

"She contacted us shortly after Jamison passed away and told us we had a grandchild. We never knew anything about this child and wondered why Jamison never mentioned him. Come to find out, she never told him. She was angry because he broke up with her to be with you. She said you broke up their family."

"So, she didn't tell Jamison he had a child because he moved on?"

"That's what she said."

"When she told us about our grandson, we were excited and wanted to see him right away."

"That's when she said she would allow us to meet him and be a part of his life if we helped her get what rightfully belonged to Jamison's son."

"A part of the estate?"

"Yes. So, we agreed to help her however we could."

"What kind of help did she want?"

"She wanted information about you and Jamison's estate. We didn't think there would be any harm in that. We weren't aware she was sending you notes and placing demands. We never would have done it if we'd known she was going to do that."

"Why did you lie to me and tell me you didn't know her?"

"She wouldn't allow us to see him under any circumstances if we told you what was going on. You have to understand we were desperate. We'd just lost Jamison and we were at odds with you, and you wouldn't let us see the triplets. We missed Jamison so much and wanted to have a connection to him."

"I wonder why she didn't want me to know."

Davore's voice broke as she said, "I don't know, but now that you know what's going on, we might not ever get to see our grandchild." Davore hung her head as sobs began to flow from her soul. Faith's heart broke as she observed the normally strong woman break down as she did. Hendrix moved to her side and hugged her close. Faith waited a few moments to allow Davore to compose herself.

"So, do you think this child is Jamison's?" Faith asked, looking between her in-laws.

"Yes, we do," Davore responded.

"How do you know that for sure?"

"Tisa showed us the DNA test results and the child is his." Davore held her hands out to her side.

"I thought you said Jamison didn't know anything about this child."

"That's what she told us," Davore explained.

"That's interesting." *If Jamison didn't know about this child, why would he participate in a DNA test?*

"You have to do the right thing and give that boy what's rightfully his," Davore pleaded.

"Umm, no," Faith said, shaking her head. "I'm not giving in to Tisa's demands. I don't know where those results came from."

"I guess you have a point."

"You should've told me about all of this. At least, I would've known where these notes were coming from."

"We wanted to be a part of the triplets' lives, so we didn't want to rock the boat any more than we had." Hendrix spoke up this time, with his arm still around his wife.

"You thought I wouldn't let you see your grandkids because you had a relationship with Tisa?"

"You were going through so much with losing Jamison, the kids being in the hospital and all that, so we weren't sure how you would react. We didn't want to cause you any more stress."

"Obviously, you don't know me well. I wouldn't keep you from them because of all of this. I'm not unreasonable."

"Maybe we do have some ideas about you that are untrue," Davore stated. "I have to admit, we were so busy being angry with you that we never really tried to get to know you. We should try a little harder to get acquainted."

"I agree. I need to do better, too. Jamison wouldn't want us treating each other like this. We're family and we need to act like it."

"You're right."

"Right now, I need some information from you. What is Tisa's phone number and address?"

"Why do you need that information?" Hendrix questioned.

"Because we're going to get to the bottom of this once and for all. We're going to get a DNA test. I need to get on with my life and I don't want this hanging over my head any longer."

Chapter 35

After she put her children to bed later that evening, Faith decided to contact Tisa. The sooner she dealt with the issue, the sooner everyone could get closure. She didn't know whether this child was Jamison's or not. However, if it turned out to be Jamison's son, she would provide an inheritance for him without question. She would also be open to a relationship between her children and their brother if she and Tisa could get along well enough to facilitate it.

Faith shook those thoughts from her mind and focused on the deciding factor... whether this was her husband's seed. She reached for her cell phone and prepared to select the number, but not before blocking her identity. The last thing Faith needed was Tisa calling her, in addition to the letters she'd been sending.

As she waited for the woman to answer, Faith rehearsed her approach to the conversation. She didn't want to anger the woman, but at the same time she felt she needed to send a clear message to Tisa that she was taking the situation seriously.

"Hello," Tisa answered.

"Hi, Tisa. This is Faith."

"Oh, do you have my money?"

"No, but I will if a DNA test proves your son is Jamison's child. I'm not the wicked stepmother you threatened to tell people I am, but I'm not a fool, either."

"If I recall, in order to do that you need a mother, a child, and a potential father. We're missing one part of that equation. So, you can make that check out to Tisa Alexander. Certified funds only, please."

Faith chuckled. "You're probably banking on us not being able to do a paternity test, but Jamison's absence isn't a problem."

"Again, where are we going to get a sample of his DNA?"

"His parents."

"Nice try. Why would they want another DNA test when they've already seen the results and accept my son as their grandson?"

"They heard what you said and saw those test results, but none of that amounts to proof that Jamison is your son's dad at all. We all just want to make sure everything is legit."

"So, what if I don't do this?"

"I don't see why you wouldn't, since you're so sure this is Jamison's child."

"Oh, it's Jamison's son."

"Why didn't you tell Jamison he had a son?"

"He didn't deserve to know once he got with you and left me hanging."

"Seems like a poor reason to deny your son a relationship with his father."

"Don't judge me. We'll take care of our samples and let you know when it's done."

"No, I'm going to be present when everyone's samples are taken. See, I don't trust you and I need to make sure you don't manipulate things."

"Suit yourself."

"I'll be in touch to set everything up."

"I can't wait."

"By the way, there's something about your story that bothers me. How is it that Jamison didn't know about this child, yet he provided a sample and signed for the testing? That doesn't make much sense."

Faith's question was met with silence. She looked at her phone's screen and realized the call had been disconnected.

***

Two weeks and three missed appointments later, Faith was still waiting for Tisa and her son to provide samples for the paternity test. She fumed at Tisa's audacity. After all of the harassment she had inflicted on Faith, she didn't even have enough courage to follow through with proving her child's paternity. Faith couldn't help but wonder if she didn't show up because she knew Jamison wasn't the child's father.

Faith changed the TV to the local news station. After the weather, the broadcaster introduced the next story.

The newscaster said, "Our next story is a sad one. A local woman is seeking support for her son from his deceased father's estate. Tisa Alexander's son was fathered by local businessman and the owner of The Lewis Agency, Jamison Lewis. Mr. Lewis passed away in an unfortunate car accident but left a large estate. The problem? Her son didn't receive any of it. Here's her story."

Faith's eyes bucked when Tisa's face appeared on the screen, prompting her to increase the volume.

"Jamison never provided a nickel to support his child. I know everyone saw him as a wonderful man because of his philanthropic efforts in the community. However, he was not quite so liberal with his own child. Since his death, I've been in touch with his widow, hoping she would understand my plight since we're both mothers. However, she also refuses to release any of her husband's estate to my son. He has just as much right to it as her children do. I don't know very much about Mrs. Lewis, but I would think she would do right by her late husband's son, even though Jamison never did. It's unfortunate, but I'm going to have to spend money I don't have to file a lawsuit to get what my son deserves."

The newscaster's face came into view. "If you'd like to help this woman raise the money she needs for legal fees, a fund has been set up. The bank's address, phone number and account number for the fund are on your screen. You will also find it on our website. Back to you, Susan."

Faith turned the television off. It was clear Tisa had no intention to tell the truth. It wasn't in her best interest to tell everyone she refused to take the steps necessary to settle the issue of paternity. She wouldn't say how Faith said she would provide whatever was fair if the child proved to be Jamison's. Tisa

195

wouldn't tell them how she attempted to extort Faith. Now, Faith felt as though she'd been played by Tisa. She mistakenly assumed the woman would handle this appropriately. Now, Faith knew she wasn't dealing with someone with good character. Tisa was a bully who would do whatever she felt she needed to do to get what she wanted, no matter who she hurt in the process.

Faith picked up her phone to make the first of two phone calls she needed to make. Her first phone call would be to her lawyer. Something needed to be done to get Tisa to end her assault on Jamison's character as well as her own. Her second phone call would be to her in-laws to let them know what Tisa was up to.

Chapter 36

It was lunchtime in the Lewis household. Faith had just spooned oatmeal into JJ's mouth when her phone rang. She looked at the phone's screen and noticed it was Davore. She answered on speakerphone as she scooped oatmeal into Mercy's and Grace's mouths.

"Hi, Davore. How are you?"

"I'm well." JJ began to squeal and kick his feet against his high chair. "What are my grandbabies doing? I can hear one of them."

"That's JJ. Apparently, I'm not scooping food into his mouth fast enough." The two shared a laugh.

"Jamison was the same way when he was that age. I couldn't keep up with him. Of course, I didn't have three of them at once, which I know makes a big difference."

"You and I know that, but JJ doesn't seem to know or care. He has to understand I can't ignore his sisters, just so I can satisfy him."

Davore laughed. "He'll learn. Soon, they'll be able to eat on their own. Then he can eat as fast as his little hands can move."

"Now, that's the truth."

"I was calling to tell you Hendrix and I spoke to Tisa. After you told us about her television appearance, we wanted some answers."

"You weren't supposed to contact her."

"I know your attorney asked us not to talk to her for now, but we just couldn't allow all of this to happen and not do anything about it, especially since we feel somewhat responsible."

"I have to admit, I wondered what she was thinking since she was threatened with legal action if she didn't stop defaming Jamison and me."

"Well, let me tell you she is livid. We surprised her when we showed up on her doorstep unannounced and demanded to see our grandson."

"Did you see him?"

"No, but we did have a long talk with Tisa."

"She still wouldn't allow you to see the boy?"

"Once we told her we weren't leaving until she told us the truth, she admitted she doesn't even have a child."

"What? You mean to tell me she took me through all of that and she was lying about Jamison having a son?"

"That's exactly what I'm telling you. We asked her why she would do such a thing. She explained that she broke up with Jamison, for another man who didn't turn out to be who she thought he was. Ultimately, I think she was driven by regret and greed."

"That's what Kardel told me. I don't know why this woman thought she could just tell me anything and I would give her what she wanted."

"I do need to tell you once again how sorry we are. We never should've believed her blindly."

"It's all behind us now."

"So it is."

"This season has been challenging, but it has shown me I possess strength I didn't even know I had."

"Yes, you do. You've been through a lot over the past year and you're still standing strong. But, know that we're here to help if you need us."

"Thank you and I'm sure I'll be taking you up on your offer."

"Well, I'm going to let you go so you can finish feeding the babies."

"Believe it or not, they're nodding off. I'll talk to you later."

Faith and Davore's phone conversation ended. She wiped each of her babies' faces and hands, before lifting them out of their high chairs one at a time and laying them upstairs in their beds. Afterward, she went to her own bedroom and laid down as well. She allowed a few tears to fall before wiping them away. Her sadness gave way to joy. Though she'd lost her husband and nearly her sanity, she was thankful for her life, family, and her friends.

Chapter 37

Evan stopped in his tracks as he entered their home. He heard what sounded like sobbing. He darted through the house, looking for Janay since she was the only other person there at the time. He went to the kitchen and didn't find her there. Finally, he located her upstairs in the guest room. Evan stood in the door for a few moments, unsure of what to do for Janay. Eventually, he sat beside her on the bed, waiting silently for her to acknowledge his presence.

After a few moments passed, Evan slipped his arm around his wife and pulled her close.

"What's going on, babe?" Evan inquired.

Janay took a couple of tissues from the box on the nightstand and wiped her face and nose with them.

"I'm scared, Evan."

"Scared of what?"

"Since we got back together, things have been going really well."

"I feel the same way. I still don't understand the tears."

"Do you remember when I asked you for some time away from the family?"

"Yes, I remember clearly."

"I'm starting to feel that way again. I'm fighting it, but I'm worried that I might give in." Janay wrung her hands.

"You don't want to be here?" Evan repositioned himself to face his wife.

"I do." Janay's voice rose. "I thought I was past that, but I'm finding out I'm not."

"What does your counselor say about this?"

"I haven't shared it with her."

Evan brushed away a tear as it rolled down Janay's face. "What can I do? Is it something I'm not doing? Please tell me. Whatever it is, I'll fix it."

"That's just it, Evan. It's not you. It's me." She touched the side of his face. "I feel a little trapped."

"I don't like the sound of that."

"I feel like I can't do the things I'd like to do because of my responsibilities. I think I'm frustrated and don't know how to deal with it."

"What is it you want to do?"

Janay smiled as she looked off into space. "There are a lot of things running through my mind, but one thing I know for sure is, I want us to have a regular date night. Oh, and I think I might want to go to college. Eventually, I want to go to Europe. See the world. Expand my horizons."

"Is that all?"

"I know that's a lot. I don't expect we'll be able to do all of that, but you asked what I wanted to do."

"We can make all of that happen. We might have to wait a little while on the world travel, but the rest we can do."

Janay smiled as she bounced on the bed. "Really?"

"Absolutely. What do you think you want to study?"

"I want to be a nurse. I want to help people."

"That's awesome, babe. Nurse Janay. I like the sound of that."

"I do, too." Janay and Evan held hands as they sat in silence. Janay smiled at her husband and said, "Thank you, honey. I feel better already."

"I'm glad you're feeling better. You have got to let me know when you're feeling frustrated. I don't ever want you to feel like you want to run away again. Just because you're a wife and mother, doesn't mean you stop being an individual with your own needs. There's no reason for either one of us to be frustrated because our personal desires aren't met. No more holding that stuff back, okay?"

"Okay. I promise to communicate better. I love you."

"I love you, too."

Chapter 38

When Faith arrived at the cemetery, she realized she wasn't sure where Jamison's gravesite was. She was so out of sorts the day he was buried, she couldn't possibly recall. She stopped by the office and one of the employees showed her exactly where it was. She thanked her and the woman left her there.

Faith pulled the collar of her coat up around her neck to shield herself from the December chill. She returned to her vehicle to obtain the blanket she kept in her car for emergencies and laid it on the ground in front of the headstone. She sat silently, allowing memories to flood her mind as tears began to flow down her cheeks.

"I know I haven't been to visit since the day we buried you here. I just couldn't bear it. I can't say it's much easier today, but I felt I needed to come." Faith brushed a few dead leaves away. "I miss you more than you can ever imagine. Things have been rough without you here to help. I'm trying to understand why you had to leave us when you did. I'm not angry, just wondering." Faith paused as she gathered herself to express the thoughts that ran through her mind. "We need you. The babies are getting big.

You'd be so proud. I'll make sure to tell them all about you, and when they get a little older, I'll bring them for a visit. Your parents and I have worked things out and hopefully we'll be able to maintain a good relationship." Suddenly Faith's mind shifted to the Tisa situation. Tisa. She shook her head as though she was shaking the memory out of her mind. "Why didn't you tell me about Tisa? She caused a big problem because she was mad about what happened between you two. It sure would've helped if I'd known about her ahead of time. I would've known the truth." Faith's quiet crying turned to sobs. She sat, touching the lettering on the stone marking her husband's final resting place. She stood and took up the blanket. "I love you, baby. I'll see you later." Faith stood, picking up her blanket and backed away from the site. She got in the car and headed toward home.

Chapter 39

The Lewis household was all decked out for the Christmas season. Poinsettias of all hues were scattered randomly throughout the house. A number of Christmas trees decorated with different themes added to the ambiance. Wreaths with lights and ornaments hung over each doorway.

Faith always loved Christmas. Seeing the children's reactions to the sights and sounds of the season caused her to love it even more. She smiled as she watched them play with both sets of grandparents and Kardel. The doorbell rang. Faith went through the foyer, which was lit with its own tree, to the front door and utilized the camera to see who was there. All she could see was several gift bags, concealing the identity of the carrier. The bags moved, revealing Macie.

"Girl, open this door. I'm trying to surprise you. Hurry up. You know my blood can't take this Michigan weather since I've been living in Georgia."

Faith laughed as she opened the door. She took the bags Macie had in her hands, leaving her capable of dragging more in from the porch. The two embraced and kissed each other's cheeks.

Macie flipped the ball on Faith's hat. "What do you have on your head?"

"You mean my Santa hat? You know I get into the Christmas spirit."

"Yeah, you've always been Miss Santa."

Faith looked at the ceiling as tears threatened her eyes. "This is my first Christmas without him. I'm trying to keep things light but it's hard, you know?" She fanned her face.

"I know." Macie took her friend in her arms again.

Faith stepped away and swiped at the tears rolling down her cheeks. "We need to stop this or I'll end up in the ugly cry."

Macie stood silent for a beat. "Where are my little stars?" Macie hung her coat on a rack in the foyer and headed further into the house.

"Everyone's in the kitchen and dining room, right now."

"Merry Christmas, everybody! How y'all doing?" Everyone responded.

Faith watched as Kardel's eyes met Macie's. She took Jamison Jr. from Kardel as he stood to greet Macie. Without words, the two embraced for what seemed like several minutes, then looked into each other's eyes. This moment made her miss her husband. She shook herself instead of allowing herself to fall into the deep grief she'd been feeling during what would normally be her favorite time of the year.

"All right. You two need to break it up." The group laughed as Hendrix ended the private party.

"It's been too long since I've seen you," Kardel stated.

"I know. Long-distance relationships are like that," Macie responded.

"Come on, Macie. We've talked about this. You know how I feel."

"I live in Georgia and you live in Michigan. We can't have the type of relationship you want."

Kardel took Macie's hands in his. "I heard you were thinking about moving back to Michigan."

"I wonder where you heard that?" Macie eyed Faith, who looked in the opposite direction.

"So, did you make a decision?" Kardel asked Macie.

"Yes, I did."

"So, are you going to tell me?" Kardel searched for Macie's eyes.

Macie took a deep breath and allowed Kardel to meet her eyes. "I decided to stay in Georgia. Even though I miss all of you, this opportunity is just what I've been praying for. I'm a little concerned about being away from Faith, but I can't put my life on hold for her, either."

"What about us? Where does that leave us?"

"Look, I like you. A lot. But, we met at the wrong time."

"Why do I feel like you're breaking up with me before we even get together?"

"I don't think long-distance relationships work. When will we spend time together?"

"You could just come back." Macie and Kardel chuckled.

"I know, but I feel like I need to give it a chance. Have you considered finding someone to manage the agency so you can expand in Georgia? That would be perfect."

"I can't leave right now. The agency needs the stability and so does Faith."

Silence permeated the room.

Macie and Kardel separated physically but maintained visual contact.

"Somebody needs to give up one of these babies. I haven't seen them in months," Macie said, breaking the uneasy silence.

Davore handed Mercy to her. "I have to check the food anyway. But, don't get too comfortable, because I'll be back for her in just a few minutes." She flicked her finger under the baby's chin.

"You get to see them all the time. Let me have some time with my goddaughter."

"I'm in line right behind you, because I don't get to see them often enough either," Vonda said.

The group of family and friends participated in lively conversation while the meal was still cooking. Hendrix approached Faith.

"Hey, is everything okay?" Hendrix asked his daughter-in-law.

"Yes, things are great. I kinda feel guilty about being happy when Jamison can't see all of this."

"I believe my son would want you to have fun and enjoy your life. He would probably be disappointed if you didn't."

"You're probably right."

"Whatever happened with Tisa?"

"Ms. Smith called me and told me Tisa admitted to making that complaint and writing those notes."

Hendrix shook his head. "People sometimes have a warped way of thinking. She needs much prayer."

"And, a new job. She violated hospital privacy policy and they were forced to let her go. I hope she gets past her bitterness so she can move on and be a better person in general."

The doorbell rang again. Hendrix said, "I'll get it." Faith followed him as he went to the door and saw who desired entry. She saw him take a deep breath and exhale. She knew this would be difficult, but she had warned everyone this moment would most likely occur. He opened the door.

"Happy holidays," Evan, Janay and the Ns said in unison, as the family knocked snow off their boots before entering the home.

"Happy holidays to you all, too." Hendrix helped them hang their coats then shook Evan's hand. "You all come on in. We'll be eating in a few minutes." Before he closed the door, there was a knock.

"Hello." Hendrix turned to see the photographer Faith hired to document the triplets' first Christmas.

"Welcome," Faith said. "You are just in time." She led the woman and her assistant to the family room where she had set up for the photo shoot. "Let me know if you need anything."

Faith looked at her watch and realized it was feeding time. She returned to the kitchen to prepare a snack to tie the children over and handed one each to Macie, Vonda, and Bill. She hoped it wouldn't put them to sleep but would keep them from getting fussy while they took pictures.

Thirty minutes later, the triplets were fed, burped and happy. The photographer announced she was ready so everyone found their way to the family room. The photographer and her assistant worked together to arrange everyone. Several shots were taken of the entire group. Then, photographs were taken of different groupings.

Finally, the family sat down for dinner. The table was spread with ham, chicken and several side dishes. Bill and Hendrix, the family patriarchs, stood to pray over the gathering and the meal. Then, Faith spoke to everyone.

"The last five months have been challenging. There's no doubt about that. But, we've all made it to this point. There were moments where I thought I wouldn't make it through. I think I was giving up, but the people in this room wouldn't allow me to drown in depression and grief. Losing Jamison was one of the worst things that could have ever happened to me. But, as I look around this table, I'm thankful. I'll miss my husband—we all will in our own way—but I've learned there is life after whatever we go through. Regardless of how bad it is, we still must find a way to live."

Faith looked around the table and realized the importance of each person sitting around the table. After Jamison's death, Faith wasn't sure who was family and who wasn't. Faith glanced at Davore and Hendrix. She now knew they were all family and though families sometimes had disagreements and might go for a period of time apart because of those disagreements, the love of true family would always prevail. Her eyes fell on Evan and Janay, who was obviously uneasy, and realized family isn't always defined by blood relationships and the most unlikely people can become a part of one's family. What she had sitting around the table with her today was a real family and not the make-believe family she once thought she had.

The Make-Believe Family
Discussion Questions

1) Evan and Faith had an emotional affair in *The Make-Believe Wives*. Once it ended and Faith married Jamison, do you think it was appropriate for them to maintain a relationship of any kind? Should Faith have disconnected from the Ns?

2) Do you think Faith was right to ban Davore and Hendrix from her home? Was Faith's peace more important than them bonding with their grandchildren?

3) On page 93, Janay says, "... this woman (Faith) required a whole different level of forgiveness Janay wasn't capable of just yet." Do different levels of forgiveness exist or is forgiveness just forgiveness?

4) Should Davore and Hendrix have expressed their concerns about Faith and Jamison's marriage?

5) Should a person ever forbid their spouse from doing something?

6) On page 160, Evan says, "... In order to inflict that type of pain on you, they have to be feeling at least that level of pain themselves." Do you agree with this statement?

7) Do you think Jamison should have told Faith about his relationship with Tisa? How much of a spouse's past should be revealed prior to getting married?

8) Janay felt she had to sacrifice her personal dreams and desires for the sake of her family. Do you agree? Why or why not?

9) Have you ever encountered a situation that was so daunting or painful that you questioned whether God was useful?

Dear Reader,

Thank you so much for reading *The Make-Believe Family*. I hope you enjoyed it. My desire is that you take away a message that will have a positive impact on your life. If I achieve that goal, I did my job. I know there are millions of other books you could spend your time reading. I am honored you chose to read one of mine.

If you liked *The Make-Believe Family*, please consider writing a review on the online retailer website of your choice. Also, visit me at my website, www.DarlissBatchelor.com. There, you'll learn about my other books, read excerpts, see video and much more. You will also have the opportunity to sign up for updates, giving you access to exclusive content, early release information, discounts and freebies.

Until the next book,

Darliss Batchelor

P.S. You can also find me on the web:
Website: www.DarlissBatchelor.com
Facebook: www.FaceBook.com/BooksByDarliss
Amazon Author Page: www.amazon.com/author/DarlissBatchelor
Goodreads: www.Goodreads.com/DarlissBatchelor

It was on a white sand beach in Cozumel, Mexico that Darliss received the call to write her first book. *Secrets* was born ten years later and she hasn't stopped. Her books, *Hell is a Skyscraper: A Trio of Novelettes, Something Else to Want,* and *The Make-Believe Wives* followed. T*he Make-Believe Family will* join her book family in the summer of 2018. Currently, her books are listed as both required and optional texts for a university-level Oral Communications class.

Walking in the footsteps of her Christian playwright grandmother, Darliss was also commissioned to write and witnessed the performance of her short play, *One Simple Yes*.

A passionate writer, Darliss desires to write stories that have a profound and lasting impact on the lives of her readers. She is committed to continue to write entertaining and inspirational fiction for years to come.

When she is not writing, she can be found spending time with her husband of over thirty years, Greg, her son, Brandon and grandson, Bentley. She also enjoys reading, cruising, Detroit Pistons basketball and watching court shows on television.

You can find more information about Darliss at her website at www.DarlissBatchelor.com.

Other books by Darliss Batchelor

Secrets
Hell is a Skyscraper: A Trio of Novelettes
Something Else to Want
The Make-Believe Wives

Available on
www.DarlissBatchelor.com